ISBN 979-8-9913942-9-1

Published by Hidden Hand Press
www.hiddenhandbooks.com

Cover picture by Diana Lamadrid

ChatEntropy:
A Novel

By T.C. Eisele

For Diana...

PART I

1

Like the blink of an eye or a sigh, another week of his life had passed without much to distinguish it from the others.

Halfway through a bottle of wine, he sits at his laptop mulling over the depressing irony of preparing to surf on the internet after 8 hours of teleworking at home.

"What else is there to do?" he thinks. "This fucking pandemic has us all trapped."

Following a sip of wine, he stares at the waiting keypad. "So, which virtual reality do I want to run away to this weekend?"

After routinely typing out "online chat sites" in the search bar, he scrolls down the list until an unfamiliar one catches his eye.

"ChatEntropy," he mutters to himself, "What kind of a name is that?"

Upon doing a quick search for the definition of "entropy," the explanation of randomness seems a welcome alternative to the isolation of being quarantined in his apartment all day, so he clicks the link and waits for a surprise.

The homepage of ChatEntropy is unexpectedly non-descript. In fact, all that's on the screen is the word "ChatEntropy" in a large, stylized font with "sign up" in a smaller typeface underneath.

At first, this minimal imagery causes him to assume he might've stumbled upon a new porn site. *Do I want to roll that way tonight?* he thinks to himself. He's certainly not adverse to taking the stick shift out for an occasional spin, in fact, he considers it an integral part of his wellness program. Yet there's something about this site that seems different, darker.

In the middle of trying to decide what to do, curiosity manages to get the upper hand and he compulsively clicks 'Sign Up."

2

"Nothing new so far," he thinks, after a pop-up window appears on the screen showing fields to type in an email address, username, and password.

He immediately enters one of his emails, yet the username field causes him to pause.

He considers for a moment what would insinuate entropy, and then, with a giggle, types in the nickname, *Nameless*."

After clicking 'Yes' on the disclaimer asking if he's over 18 years of age, the next prompt that appears is a request to connect with the camera in his computer. After he agrees, the screen goes black again until a new screen appears with a button marked 'Start' down in the lower right corner.

Sometimes, clicking the cursor on a computer can be as easy as making an impulse buy on Amazon. Other times, it can be as hard as standing on the high board for the first time and looking down at the swimming pool below. Nameless' mind is hovering somewhere between the two when he whispers, "Fuck it," and decisively clicks 'Start'.

3

Once he's connected to live chat, Nameless notices the 'Start' button suddenly change to 'Next'.

"Don't forget, that's your escape hatch," he quietly reminds himself. "If there's anything you don't want to deal with, just 'Next' it.

A moment later, he's facing a Gen Z e-boy double thumbing their phone.

"Hey," says the young man, without looking up from texting.

"How's it going?" replies Nameless.

"Sorry," says the e-boy, as he continues typing like a fiend. "I'm checking to see if any Sheesh influencers are currently on site. That's where all the snacks would be."

When he's done, the e-boy looks at Nameless with a knowing grin. "That's why we're here, right? To follow the river of likes to the source."

"Like Stanley and Livingstone," replies Nameless.

Apparently not a history buff, the e-boy mutters, "Yeah, whatever," as he's distracted by another text.

After reading the new message, he suddenly announces, ", I gotta bounce. A spot just opened up in a chat with "GenZerious."

"Who?" thinks Nameless, as he suddenly finds himself once again looking at a blank screen.

4

Nameless' next chat buddy is a smiling young man with brown tousled hair.

"How's it going mate?" he asks, in a crisp British accent.

"It's going," answers Nameless.

"Have you been on here long?"

"Long enough to be 'next'ed for not being a snack," replies Nameless, as he takes in the young Jude Law clone in front of him.

"I don't know," says the Brit with a smirk. "You look snacky enough for me."

"I think my previous chat buddy was looking for a she/her."

"I wouldn't penalize you for not being a she/her," says the young Brit jokingly, "Maybe for not putting a condom over the NJOY wand if we were sharing, but never for not being a woman."

Not knowing what an "NJOY wand" is, Nameless figures he'd be better off not asking.

"Are you on this site often?" asks the Brit.

"Nope, this is my first time,"

They both stare at each other.

"So, what are you looking for?" he asks Nameless.

"Not the meaning of life, but not an excuse for it either."

"Cheers to that" says the Brit. After hesitating, he bluntly adds, "I'm not into the rough stuff. Just about anything else is okay."

Before Nameless can reply, the Brit continues. "I'm sorry if I'm being too cheeky, but it's just so tiring beating around the bush. I usually do Dirty Roulette on Friday night, and those blokes cut right to the chase."

"No worries," says Nameless.

Smiling now like he's suddenly hit the jackpot; the Brit confidently forges ahead. "The problem with

Dirty Roulette is that there's always the same type of trade on it. Been there, done that, you know?"

When Nameless doesn't respond, the Brit just keeps going.

Since this site is new, I decided to see what was going on here tonight?"

"Whatever satisfies," says Nameless.

"And what satisfies you?"

"Well, for starters I'm on team hetero."

"Are you sure?" says the Brit, with a playful smile. "If there isn't a bi-curious urge lurking around in you somewhere, then why are we still talking?"

"I talk with men all the time," replies Nameless. "It's a human thing."

"Why don't we take a look at each other's junk and then decide if you'd like to do more than just talk?"

After noticing Nameless glance toward the lower right where the 'Next' button is, the Brit's cock-sure expression suddenly changes into a look of mock apology.

"It's been super cool chit-chatting with you," he says quickly, "but I really think it would be best if I carried on elsewhere."

Before Nameless can react, he once again finds himself 'next'ed.

5

Nameless's next chat buddy is a broad-faced, smiling young Mexican dude.

"*Hola*. Uh, no...Hay-lo," he says.

"How's it going?" asks Nameless.

"I sorry. My Ing-lish no good.

"Okay," replies Nameless, not knowing what else to say.

"You pratica, uh, no...prac-tis with me?"

Before Nameless can respond, the back of a little head with long black hair appears on the screen right in front of the young man's chest. Looking down at the head of hair, the young man asks, "*Que?*" and then assists a cute little Mexican girl onto his lap.

"*Yo tengo hambre*," she says to the man.

The little girl then turns and looks at Nameless on the screen. "*Quien es*?" she asks.

Nameless is now looking at two brown smiling faces.

"*Mi hija,*" explains the young man to Nameless. "Uh, no. My dow-ter," he says, trying to correct himself in English.

I can be an ugly American or an awkward one, thinks Nameless.

He opts for awkward, which for him means abruptly 'next'ing someone else for a change.

"Oh well, *adios* is *adios,*" he thinks to himself, as he says the same to the now empty screen in front of him.

6

Next up is a young black man with corn-rowed hair, expensive shades, and the aplomb of a hit man.

"Whaddup?" he says grimly.

Before Nameless can reply, a raucous voice from somewhere behind the young man shouts, "Y'all come across a honey yet?"

The Dude in shades turns to the voice and shouts back, "Nah."

"Then move on, blood," urges the voice, "we need to be partying. No time for nothin else."

"Chill and let me see what's shakin', Aw-ite?" Shades then turns back to Nameless and sullenly asks, "You know where the bitches be on this site?

"Not really," says Nameless, after which he finds himself once again looking at a blank screen.

7

Not being a stranger to anonymous online chat rooms, Nameless continues to patiently slog through a few more dull, meaningless encounters as he works on the bottle of wine.

After a while, he finally admits to himself out loud, "If I don't have at least one semi-interesting exchange within the next three turns, I'm outta here. Maybe there's a good movie on the cable?"

After hitting 'Start' again, Nameless finally encounters his first woman.

With a user name of "Betty," the 20-something, nubile young beauty in front of him has long, blonde hair, full lips, and a generically pretty face reminiscent of the Betty character from the Archie comics.

Wow, she's a real cutie, he thinks, as he tries to say hello as nonchalantly as possible.

"Hi" she replies, with a smile like a cheesy tooth whitening advert. "What are you up to tonight?"

"Just enjoying some wine after another week of teleworking," explains Nameless, raising his glass.

The young lady reaches off screen and brings back a mug that's holding something steaming. "I'm enjoying a spot of herbal tea," she says, and giggles.

"To the weekend!" toasts Nameless.

As they each take a sip of their beverage, Nameless tries to check out his new chat partner on the sly.

Very girl-next-door sexy, he thinks to himself. *A little ditsy too, but I can work with that.*

"So, do you do much online chatting?" she asks.

"From time to time."

"This is my first time on this site," she says, "so I wasn't sure what to expect. It didn't say very much about what kind of people are on here."

"I think that's the point," replies Nameless. "Each chat is supposed to be a surprise, isn't it? For better or worse."

"Well, you're my very first person and you seem nice. Where are you from?"

"New York."

"I've never been there, but I've heard it's dangerous. Is that true?"

"That depends. Statistically it's not as dangerous as say, Cincinnati, Ohio.

"Really? I'm from Dayton and I've never heard that."

"I guess it just goes to show how you can't believe anything the media says."

"Amen to that," she replies with a warm smile.

"What brings you here on a Friday night?" asks Nameless.

"I'm not sure. I just felt guided here," she looks away with an embarrassed smile, "I can't believe I just said that. Ignore me, I'm a crazy person."

"That's okay. What do you mean by guided?"

She looks at him with the suspicion of a little girl. "You're not making fun of me, are you?"

"Oh no," replies Nameless. "There's been plenty of times I've done things because of a feeling, or whatever."

"Really?" she says, with a relieved smile.

"Sure. Go ahead. I'm all ears."

"I can't always explain exactly how it works," she says, with a serious expression, "but deep down inside I always feel like spirit is directing me to wherever I'm supposed to go,"

"I can believe that," says Nameless. "In fact, I'm sensing there's a reason why we've met tonight."

"Really? That's great! Maybe our angels were talking together before this?"

"I must admit, I'm not really very in touch with that kind of stuff," he says. "Not that I don't believe in it, I'm just not as sensitive, or attuned, as someone like you."

"Thank you," she replies. I get it from my grandma. She's had the Archangel Michael appear to hear several times. She's really amazing. So spiritual."

"I bet she is."

After a few more minutes of conversation, the beatific smile that had been plastered across the face of this apparently pleasant young woman unexpectedly changes into something more serious as Nameless breaks for a sip of wine.

"Do you really believe there's a reason why we've met," she asks.

"Absolutely," he replies, "there's most definitely something at work tonight that's brought us together."

"That's what my angel is telling me. But they're also saying there's something else I need to ask you that's very important."

She now stares at him with a set, determined expression.

"Of course," says Nameless, as he puts down his wine glass and sits back to hear what her angel has on its mind.

In a voice now suddenly filled with unexpected spiritual fervor, the young blonde challenges Nameless and demands, "Are you willing to accept the Lord Jesus Christ as your personal savior?"

Feeling both surprised and a bit deflated at the same time, Nameless instinctively maneuvers the cursor toward NEXT and immediately removes her from his screen.

"No one expects the Spanish Inquisition," he grumbles to himself, as the site reloads a new chat window.

8

Nameless' next chat is a balding, round-face, businessman type that looks like he could be the father of the previous blonde. Yet at the same time there is something lurking in the expression behind his wire rim glasses that suggests his thoughts about her would be more lascivious than paternal.

"What are you into?" he asks quietly.

"What do you mean?"

The man leans in a little closer, "You know, what are you into?"

"Raindrops on roses and whiskers on kittens," says Nameless glibly.

A humorless laugh dribbles out of the man's mouth.

"C'mon, why are you on this site?" he asks.

"To meet interesting new friends," replies Nameless.

“Exactly. What sort of friends? Women? Men? Something else?”

“What if I said something else?”

“Is there an age range you’re looking for?” asks the Man.

“Well, when you sign up here it says you have to be 18, right?”

“Maybe,” says the Man, grinning like Nameless imagines a rat would.

“Maybe?” replies Nameless, as his face recoils in disgust. “Wow, either this is entrapment, or you’re a fucking pervert.”

“Hey, be cool,” says the Man.

“I don’t think I will,” replies Nameless. “These fingers of mine are itching to make the vice squad my next chat buddy.”

9

As he takes a time out to down what's left in his wine glass, the idea of watching a movie on Netflix is starting to seem very appealing to Nameless.

However, after pouring some more *vino*, he instead moves the cursor on the screen back to 'Start'.

Once he's connected to another chat, Nameless finds that he's now looking into an empty room.

"What the fuck is this?" he mutters.

It takes a second for him to realize what he's looking at, but when he does, Nameless quietly exclaims, "Holy shit!"

He now starts to look back and forth between what's on the screen and what's behind him in his space.

"That's my fucking apartment!" he blurts out. "The only thing that's missing is me!"

For a few confusing moments, Nameless tries to wrap his mind around what's happening. Yet before he can make sense of anything, the image on his computer screen is suddenly replaced by a Google 404 service message stating, "the site you are looking for cannot be found."

10

On waking the next morning, Nameless turns over in bed and looks nervously at his computer on the other side of the room.

When the memory of seeing his apartment on the screen the night before pops into his head, he slowly rolls on his back and stares up at the ceiling.

"That shit was like something out of the horror flick *Oculus*," he says quietly to himself.

After a few more moments of anxious and paranoid reflection, Nameless opts to put the matter out of his head and instead gets up and starts to get ready to go out into the covid world for some essential items.

"Maybe it was just a combination of the wine and cabin fever," he thinks, as he stands over the toilet and listens to the water works.

Once he's washed and dressed, Nameless heads out for a few hours to wait in the street with his masked neighbors and pick up what he needs from the market and liquor store.

The nearest Trader Joe's is across town, and as Nameless walks along the deserted Manhattan streets he can't help but think of the movie "I Am Legend."

At least Robert Neville had a dog, he thinks, while noting the absence of anyone else in the immediate vicinity.

It isn't until 10 blocks later when he arrives at Trader Joe's that Nameless finally encounters other humans. The line of masked and socially distanced people waiting outside the store wraps around the block, and it takes over an hour before he gets in.

Once inside the store, it's like having your own private market. There's no more than one person in any aisle, no waiting at the checkout, and no idle small talk at the register. As he watches the masked young clerk pack the groceries in silence, Nameless finds himself almost missing the mindless platitudes he would have exchanged with this young fellow in the past

By contrast, the liquor store is a much faster errand. The line is far shorter, and when it's Nameless' turn an employee asks what he wants, takes his credit card, and returns a couple of minutes later with the bottles of wine and a receipt.

The remainder of his walk home through the deserted streets passes like a daydream, and as Nameless enters his apartment building he reflects on the journey. Minus the people that were waiting outside of Trader Joe's and the liquor store, he calculates that he only passed about 5 people during the whole trip.

"I Am Legend, the prequel," he thinks, as he unlocks the door to his apartment and enters.

Later, after dinner and a few drinks, he starts looking online for a movie. As he scrolls over the picks on Netflix, Nameless' mind instead returns to what he saw the night before on ChatEntropy.

"That could *not* have been my apartment," he thinks, yet another part of him insists on playing devil's advocate and counters, "You know that fucking place looked *exactly* like your apartment."

Some of the mysteries we become obsessed with are paths to self-destruction, yet others, no matter how frightening or uncomfortable, are the pathways that lead us to our destiny. As Nameless turns off the TV and decides to fire up his laptop, he's not only compulsively hoping to find that room again from last night, he's also looking to reclaim a sense of normalcy that lately has become conspicuous in its absence.

11

If Nameless had thought that going back into ChatEntropy was going to be like Neo taking the red pill in the Matrix, his first chat puts an end to that notion.

"Are you a patriot?" demands a white dude in a MAGA hat who has a thick beard, menacing eyes, and a neck like a linebacker.

"Are you Q?" asks Nameless.

With a fierce look, the man suddenly holds up a Ruger SR9 automatic pistol and points it at the screen.

"You better run now you fucking woke, lib-tard, child-molesting cocksucker! The Revolution is coming and traitors like you are gonna suffer the wrath of real Americans!"

12

While wondering if that MAGA dude actually thought he could shoot through the screen, Nameless is suddenly confronted with a new chat buddy in the form of a strange looking yet fetching young Asian woman.

"Hello," she breathes, with her eyes communicating a mixture of raw sex and cabaret comedy.

"Hi," replies Nameless.

"I've been waiting to encounter a handsome young man like you" she says, gently biting her voluptuous bottom lip with some very pearly white teeth.

"Aren't you a sweet talker?" counters Nameless.

"I'm sweet in a lot of ways."

"I bet. The darker the berry, the sweeter the juice."

"Aren't you a funny one! You know intelligent people really turn me on. I'm what you would call a sapiosexual. Do you know what that is?"

After hesitating a moment, Nameless smiles broadly at her and then says very slowly and deliberately, "Fib-o-na-cci sequence."

"Ooh, I love it," she giggles.

Despite his initial intention to only focus on finding that mystery room from last night, Nameless can't help but be turned on by this young lady's Lorna Lust routine.

"I have a question," she says, with a sly smile.

"And what would that be?" asks Nameless.

"Could you please empty your pockets for me?"

"I'd love to, but right now my pockets are already empty."

"Could you please check and make sure?

At first, he hesitates, but when she says, "Feel around in there for a little bit, maybe you'll find something unexpected?" he decides to go all in.

At that point, the Woman tilts her screen down to reveal her slightly open bathrobe that offers a glimpse of her firm, golden skin between its folds.

Inspired, Nameless starts to search in his pockets and neighboring anatomy with a deepening enthusiasm.

"I don't see your hands," she says. "Does that mean you're feeling around those pockets?"

"Perhaps."

"Per-haps?" She giggles. "I bet you've discovered you have a roll of quarters down there, don't you?"

"I think I could change a few bills for you."

"I bet you could. But before you do, I'd like to show you something that might just send those quarters rolling all over the floor."

She now stands up so that the width of her hips fills the screen.

"Are you shaved down there?" asks Nameless.

"Why don't you see for yourself," she says, fully parting her robe to reveal a totally manscaped and very erect cock.

As the shock of what he's looking at scorches his retina, Nameless desperately scrambles with the cursor to try and click 'Next'.

"Hey baby boy," taunts the person on the other side of the screen, "take a walk on the wild side. You know you want to."

13

Still rebounding from an image he'll never be able to unsee, Nameless desperately hits the 'Next' button and is quickly confronted by another chat partner.

"Hi, my name is Lady Babalon, would you be interested in a magical tarot reading?"

Feeling stunned and overwhelmed, Nameless doesn't respond, thus giving this pleasingly plump, yet very attractive wannabe witch the space to continue.

"I took the liberty of pulling a random card just before we connected," she says, revealing the tarot card of "*The Lovers.*"

After letting him get a good look at the card, she continues, "I feel this is a very profound card for your future, though I don't necessarily think it's referring to its most obvious meaning. Instead, I think you should take note of how the naked man in the image is looking at the naked woman, while the woman is looking up at the Angel. The naked man is your logical mind, while the naked woman symbolizes your psychic and emotional self. The Angel above them represents enlightened consciousness, thus making me feel there's something you're very confused about spiritually and you're trying to ask your higher self for guidance."

As she prattles on, Nameless stares at her blankly, thankful she's not swinging a big, shaved dick in front of his face.

"I think you need an uncrossing spell to open you up," she says. "I can do that for you, or you can do it for yourself. All you need is a white candle and some Citrus oil. It'll help release the negative energy that I'm sensing all around you."

At this point, Nameless closes his eyes and in frustration shouts at the screen, "Abracadabra, Now you will disappear!"

After hitting the 'Next'button, he then reaches out, closes the laptop, and puts an abrupt end to a very short, yet very strange second evening on ChatEntropy.

Sunday

14

While Sunday is traditionally thought of as the day God set aside for us to rest from our labors, it offered no reprieve to Nameless. On this sabbath afternoon, he instead decides to forego tradition and prepares to dive back into the fray on ChatEntropy.

Like Lot looking back at his impetuous wife, Nameless needs to go back once more and verify the weirdness of actually seeing his empty apartment before being able to move on.

As a cold, steady rain falls outside his window, he anxiously waits for the 'Start' button to appear, and when it does, he hits it without hesitation.

Much to his surprise, the first chat encounter of the day turns out to be the Muppet Elmo.

"Hey dude, how they hangin'?" squeaks Elmo.

"They're fine. How are you doing Elmo?"

"Ready for some hot chat. What are you into, chicks or dicks?"

"My, my, Elmo you do get to the point, don't you?"

"Wait a minute, are you one of those non-binary types?"

"You mean you want to know if my taste includes puppets?"

"I want to know if you like taking it up the corn hole, you jerk-off?"

"Elmo, I'm shocked. Do you talk like that to the kids on Sesame Street?"

"What the fuck do you care? Don't talk to me like you're my friend. You're just another lonely mo-fo looking for a jerk buddy."

"Says someone presenting himself to the world as a hand puppet. Are you using the other hand to whack off?"

"Eat me!" shrieks Elmo, as Nameless suddenly finds himself looking at a blank screen.

"There go my childhood memories," Nameless mutters, while waiting for his next chat buddy to appear on the screen.

15

The next person that appears to Nameless is a square jawed, jumbo size individual wearing a New York Football Giants cap and jersey.

"Is it only me?" he bellows, "or is anyone else out there pissed off that the NFL is letting this bogus, Fauci-created pandemic stop America from seeing football on a Sunday afternoon?"

Nameless curbs his immediate instinct to hit "Next," and instead waits to hear what else this ignorant bohunk has to say. Maybe he's joking, and he'll be funnier than Elmo was?

"Football is more important to America than a few weak people getting sick," says Mr. Giant. "Did they ever suspend games or impose fascist mask-and-vaccine mandates during flu season? Fuck no! That's because..."

Unable to wait any longer for the miracle of an intelligent statement, Nameless calmly hits 'Next'.

16

Nameless now finds himself facing a pale-skinned teenage boy who looks like he could use a shower. His long, dirty hair covers one of his eyes, with the exposed side of his face exhibiting a soft, ghostlike pallor to it, much akin to someone who doesn't go outdoors very often.

"Hey," says the boy softly.

"Hey," replies Nameless.

A long moment of silence ensues, making it seem like they're a pair of strangers on an after-hours bus going where no one else seems to be headed.

"How old are you?" asks Nameless, finally ending the quietude.

"What does it matter?" answers the kid, with a pinch of sullenness.

"Do your parents know you're doing this?"

"You don't have to worry, they're not here."

"I'm not worried, I'm just wondering why you're here?" says Nameless.

"I'm looking for someone," he says.

"Here?"

"Why not, *you're* looking for someone here. Maybe we're looking for each other and we don't know it yet?"

"I'm not looking for someone that doesn't look old enough to drink," says Nameless.

"I could probably drink you under the table, motherfucker," he replies, suddenly sounding much more like an adult.

"What?"

Before this kid can say anything else, a loud noise arises from the background of wherever he is, followed by the sound of a male voice. Nameless can't make out what this other person is saying, but they're definitely yelling, and it causes the kid to turn around. When he looks back at Nameless, he seems very afraid.

"I gotta go," he says.

17

For the next couple of hours, Nameless goes through a string of rapid encounters starring a whole motley crew of ChatEntropy specters.

At one point, he even gets a little philosophical, thinking to himself, "I guess ChatEntropy is a lot like life, you keep going, yet even without hope, the pain and the frustration are still better than nothing at all."

When the evening finally arrives, Nameless resorts to wine. He decides on an Oregon Pinot Noir from his collection, and after uncorking it, he grabs one of the two 99-cent store wine glasses in the kitchen cabinet and heads back to the computer.

"This should make things a little easier," he thinks. That is, until he accidently spills some wine near his computer while filling his glass.

While trying to gingerly clean up the little bit of *vino* that splashed on his keyboard, Nameless accidently activates the NEXT button. To his numb surprise, the new screen that pops up reveals the same image of his empty apartment that he saw the night before.

"Jesus H. Christ," he mutters, "I'm back!"

Tossing away the paper towel in his hand, Nameless plops down in his chair and stares intently at the image on the screen.

With a full bottle of wine ready to back him up, as far as he's concerned, he has everything he needs to maintain a vigil until either his reality, or the one on the screen blinks first.

18

Just as he's about to finish the wine in his glass, Nameless hears the sound of a door closing in the scene depicted on his screen. After looking over his shoulder and seeing the door to his bathroom wide open, he turns back to the apartment on the screen.

As his eyes search the space in front of him, he eventually hears another sound, like someone rummaging around, yet no one appears on the screen.

Twenty-four hours ago, he would have been a nervous wreck about this, but now, something else inside of him has taken over and he watches the computer screen with the concentration of a hawk.

After a while, Nameless thinks he sees what seems to be a portion of a figure moving around in the background.

A second later, it disappears.

There's nothing for a while, then, without warning, the lower half of a figure reappears in a corner of the screen and walks across the far end of the room from right to left.

This is followed by the noise of things being shuffled around or put away, yet Nameless is unable to pick up any further movement on the screen.

When he finally notices that he's been in the same position for so long that his back and neck are starting to ache, Nameless gingerly shifts his posture in the chair.

The next thing he knows, the figure he thought he saw before is now in front of the screen, but they're so close that all Nameless can see is a blur of their clothes.

It isn't until this person sits down and looks directly at him that Nameless is finally able to see them clearly, at which point all he can do is stare in stunned silence as his exact double sits there staring back at him.

19
(Months Later)

As the Managing Agent tries one key after another on the ring he's holding, his Assistant looks down the hall toward the elevator bank.

"Of course it's going to be the last fucking key I try," says the Agent, as the cylinder of the lock finally turns over. Once he opens the door, the two men find themselves confronted by a stuffy, dusty apartment.

"How long has this place been vacant?" asks the Assistant.

"I've lost track," replies the Agent, as he searches for the light switch by the front door and turns it on. "According to the court, it's only been vacant since last week when our petition to seize the premises was ruled on by the judge. He scrunches up his face and looks around, "we really need to open a window, it smells like something died in here."

"Yeah," replies the Assistant, as he walks to the windows lining the opposite wall. After pulling one of them open, he starts to aimlessly stroll around the main room of the small apartment. “How come we couldn’t seize this place earlier,” he asks. “There must have been some pretty serious arrears.”

“It was complicated,” says the Agent. “The guy had everything on autopay, so we kept getting the rent until his money ran out. By the time he had accumulated enough arrears to start proceedings, the eviction moratorium for Covid was still in effect. At that point, it took months to get to court. What’s weird though is that we don’t know what happened to him.

“What do you mean?” asks the Assistant.

“He disappeared. No one could find him.”

“Did you contact the cops?”

“Of course. He owed us back rent.”

“I don’t understand. If we rented him the unit, he had to have given us traceable documentation. Wasn’t there a work number, an emergency contact, or even a co-signer? There had to be some way to track him down. I mean he wasn’t Jason Bourne, was he?”

"Oh my God," says the Agent with mock surprise, "we should've had you here back then to figure it all out for us." Now suddenly serious, "Of course we had his contact info, Einstein. It's just that everything turned out to be a dead end."

"Really?"

"No, I'm just saying that, so you won't think you're smarter than me."

The Assistant gives him a puzzled look.

Rolling his eyes, the Agent continues, sounding like it pains him to. "His parents are deceased, and no other family was listed. According to his employer, he just stopped working remotely one day. When he didn't return their calls, one of his friends from work came out to see what was going on. The same friend eventually reported our tenant missing and he hasn't been seen since. As far as the cops are concerned, the guy just vanished. End of story."

"Wow," says the Assistant, as he starts to look around the apartment. "All of his stuff is still here."

"Yeah, we'll have to put it all down in the basement for 30 days before we can legally trash anything."

“Look at this,” says the Assistant, walking over to a small desk where there’s an ergonomic chair and an open laptop computer.

“It’s still plugged in,” he says, pointing at the computer. He turns to his boss, but the Agent is now busy texting someone. After mulling something over in his mind for a second, the Assistant mutters, “If the electricity is still on the computer should be on too.” He then leans over and taps the space bar on the dusty keyboard.

When the computer doesn’t come on immediately, he turns back to his boss, but the Agent is still texting on his phone.

When the Assistant looks back at the computer, he is amazed to see that the screen is starting to come on, yet when he looks back at his boss in anticipation, he sees that he’s still busy.

Once the computer is fully up, it shows a screen saver depicting a mysterious, foggy landscape along with a password field.

The Assistant’s disappointment at seeing the need for a password is interrupted by his boss suddenly announcing, “We need to dig up the Super. A crew has to get in here and clean the place up right away.

It needs a paint job, the floors should be buffed, change the locks, whatever. Now that we have the unit back, we need to get it on the market asap. Time is money."

Even though he's still thinking about how to break into the computer on the desk, the Assistant nevertheless nods in agreement. He then changes the subject and asks his boss, "Do you think this tenant died of covid?"

"Who knows?"

"That's sad," says the Assistant, as he and the Agent turn to exit the apartment.

"What's sad is that this unit is collecting dust when we could be collecting money," says the Agent, clicking off the light and then locking the door behind them.

Once they're gone, the light from the laptop continues to emit an eerie glow into the shadowy apartment. After a few moments, the image on the screen begins to flicker, until it eventually changes to that of Nameless, who sits there staring blankly into the space where he used to live.

PART II

20

Two days after first being shown the place by his boss, Marshal "Marsh" Simon is back in the apartment with both the Super and a porter to clear out Nameless' belongings. Marsh had been assisting his boss, Sal, for over a year now, and this is going to be his first chance at supervising the preparation of a rental unit by himself. Although he feels a little nervous about what's in store, it's not because he isn't up to the task. On the contrary, over the last year and a half Marsh has learned his lessons well. He's also learned that Sal can be a real ballbuster, meaning that there's a pretty good chance his increased responsibilities will probably serve to make his boss even more of a control freak than he currently is. Yet, as the workers busy themselves with bagging up the items in the apartment, Marsh's mind is not entirely occupied with either Sal or what it will take to renovate the space.

Besides his new responsibilities, Marsh can't help but be intrigued by the mysterious disappearance of the previous tenant. In fact, after first hearing about it from Sal on their initial visit to the space, Marsh has been turning it over in his imagination ever since. The idea of someone literally disappearing into thin air during what amounted to a modern version of the plague held a very Poe-like, gothic allure for Marsh.

As a result, while the workers continue gathering up the stuff in the apartment, Marsh decides to commandeer the laptop computer that had been left behind and personally bring it to the basement storage room himself. Since the law dictates that's where everything must go for the next thirty days, he wants to make sure that he has sole access to what will obviously help him find out something about who the previous tenant is, and perhaps, what might have happened to him.

21

Over the next couple of weeks, the work in the apartment goes surprisingly well. Even though it seems like Sal is constantly looking over his shoulder, Marsh manages to maintain his composure, and toward the end of the second week, his boss is already talking about listing the space by the first of the month.

With a major coup now in sight, and the weekend ahead, Marsh decides to celebrate by rewarding himself ahead of time with the computer down in the basement. "Nobody's going to be checking on any of that stuff before it gets thrown out next week," he tells himself, "meaning I could take it now and it'll never even be missed."

22

When the weekend finally arrives, Marsh is up early on Saturday morning. After having a quick breakfast, he logs into the company database from home to see what he can dig up about the tenant who disappeared. A week ago, he wouldn't have dared to do this, but since Sal is on the verge of approving the unit to go on the market, Marsh rationalizes what he's about to do as performing research on a listing.

The previous tenant's name was Douglas Morrison. When he signed the lease, Mr. Morrison was 27 years old and employed as a Content Writer at an online media company with an office in Manhattan. His credit check, previous landlord, and employer references were all fine, although Sal had been right about there being no family or emergency contacts. As Marsh continues reading the file, he is surprised to see the name and phone number of the person who reported Morrison missing to both the landlord and police. "What's his connection to Morrison?" wonders Marsh. The name of the guy who sounded the alarm is Gregory Hallas, and he worked with Morrison at the media company. "It's not all the time you see someone interested in what happens to a co-worker outside of the job, " thinks Marsh. After taking down Mr. Hallas's number, Marsh goes online to check if Morrison had any of the usual social media profiles most people sign up for As expected, it turned out he was listed on Facebook, Instagram, and LinkedIn, although after an investigation of each it was obvious that he had done nothing more than the bare bones of setting them up. There were no profile pictures, few posts, and almost no personal info on any of the sites, except the name of his employer on LinkedIn. By all appearances, it looked like Mr. Douglas Morrison was intentionally staying on the downlow.

23

Expecting a voicemail, Marsh is surprised when someone answers Gregory Hallas' phone.

"Hello?" says a well-spoken, yet wispy young man's voice.

"Hi, is this Gregory Hallas?"

"Who's calling?"

"If this is Mr. Hallas, my name is Marsh Simon. I work for Copperfield Properties and I'm the Assistant Managing Agent of the building where your friend Douglas Morrison used to live."

"This is Gregory. How can I help you?"

"I'm calling to ask you some questions about Mr. Morrison. It's in our records that you were the co-worker that reported him missing. You also filed a missing person's report with the police."

"That's right. What is it exactly that you'd like to know?"

"I'm not sure. I guess whatever you can tell me about Mr. Morrison, along with anything you might be able to share regarding the circumstances around his disappearance."

"I already shared what I know with the police. I thought you said you worked for the landlord that owns the building he lived in?"

"I *do* work for the landlord, but I'm also interested when a tenant in one of my buildings disappears. From what I understand, the police aren't really pursuing the matter anymore and I'm kind of annoyed by that. I mean if I disappeared under mysterious circumstances I would certainly hope that someone would be motivated to find out what the hell happened to me."

When there's a momentary silence on the line, Marsh starts to worry that he might have come on too strong. Yet, just as he's about to start apologizing, Hallas responds.

"To tell you the truth, that's pretty much the way I've felt about it from the beginning. I only knew Doug from work, but he was a decent guy and it's creepy when someone you know just disappears and the police only seem to have a limited interest."

"I'm glad to hear you say that. I don't want to invade your privacy, but I'd like to try and find out more about Mr. Morrison's, I mean Doug's, disappearance."

"Sure, I get it," says Gregory, "but like I said, I didn't really know Doug that well and I've already told the police everything I know. I guess it wasn't enough for them to do anything."

"I know this is tough, but anything you could tell me about his interests, his activities, anything."

After a short silence, Gregory replies, "Like I said, I only knew Doug from work, so the first thing I'd have to say is that he was a pretty decent writer. I know that because I had to edit a lot of his work and he just had a way of putting things that made you want to continue reading. Personally, he could be dry, and a bit sarcastic, but it always seemed playful. Some of the stuff that came out of him was pretty funny, and pretty outrageous. A couple of times before the pandemic, a few of us went out for drinks after work and Doug showed he definitely had a wild side."

"What do you mean?" asks Marsh.

"Well, he didn't really do anything crazy, but he did like his wine. There was one time when he hit on this really exotic girl at a bar we went to. To tell you the truth, I was a little surprised to see how smooth he was. I mean this girl was pretty outrageous, you know, piercings, tattoos, sort of dangerous looking, but Doug just flowed with it. He goofed about it after she left and said her soul reminded him of his mother. We all laughed, but I thought that was a strange thing to say."

After a grunt of acknowledgement, Marsh then asks, "Do you know anything about what Doug did with himself outside of work? Did he have a girlfriend, hobbies?"

"I really don't know. Sometimes he'd mention that he did this or that over the weekend, but other than referring to a chick he met while doing it, or maybe a guy he once knew, he never mentioned anyone by name. It didn't really seem like he was in any sort of serious relationship."

Gregory pauses for a second. "I mean I didn't even know he was an only child, or that both his folks are dead until I had to ask HR for his records to file a missing person's report. To be honest, I was also a little shocked when I found out that I was the only one who had approached the cops to say he was missing."

After a moment of silence, Marsh continues, "I tried looking him up, but it didn't seem like he had any sort of online presence. Do you know anything?"

"You mean like a website or a Facebook profile?"

"Exactly! Anything he might have shared with you."

"There isn't really anything I can think of, "says Gregory. "Except for those couple of times we went out with coworkers, I don't really know what Doug did in his private life, online or otherwise."

"Okay, I get it." After a pause, Marsh continues, "It turns out there's also another reason for my call. Doug's computer was left behind in the apartment. After 30 days it becomes the landlord's property, so I was thinking about having a tech friend of mine go through it and see if there are any clues regarding Doug's online activity. I'm thinking that might shed some light on his disappearance. Since it doesn't appear like he has any other family or friends either of us are aware of, would you have any objections to me doing that?"

"Not at all," says Gregory. "Although you'd think the cops would have thought of that.

"It doesn't look like it," replies Marsh. "The computer was still sitting on his desk plugged in and covered with dust."

"Are you going to try and find him?" asks Gregory.

"I don't know. I'm going to try to do what I can. I mean I have no illusions about being an investigator, but there is something about all this that has managed to get under my skin. Maybe what happened to Doug is making me realize some things about life, and myself, that I need to get to the bottom of."

"I felt weird too when it happened," confesses Gregory. "Maybe this call is making me realize that I still sort of feel that way. Like you said, if Doug can just disappear without a trace, then it can happen to any of us. That's pretty scary."

"Yeah, it is."

Following that moment of reflection by both men, Marsh senses that it's time to end the call.

"Well, thanks for everything," he says. "I don't know where any of this is going, but I will try to stick with it as long as I can."

"Yeah, thanks for calling," says Gregory. "I wish you luck and if I come across anything that might help, I'll save your number and give you a ring." After a pause he adds, "For what it's worth, it's a good thing you're doing."

"Thanks," says Marsh, and hangs up.

24

Marsh didn't remember the last time he had spoken to Tank; all he knew was that it had been a long time. As the phone rang, he reflected on his old friend and their youth in the wilds of Queens.

"Hey Tank, what's up?"

"Hey Marsh, is that you?" says a deep, intelligent-sounding voice on the other end of the line. "I thought you died."

"I did. I'm just calling to haunt you. How's it going, Tank?"

"Shit, nobody's called me that in a minute.

"Hey, you'll always be Tank to me."

"And you'll always be the guy who turned down a Knick's playoff ticket to go out with Madame Clitoris."

"Her name was Madeline. You had the hots for her too, but I guess we all have different destinies."

"Touché Mr. Marsh. So, what have you been up to?

"I am currently working as a managing agent for a landlord."

"A landlord? Nice. Everyone should know a landlord. To what do I owe this twist of fate?"

"You're my favorite computer geek."

"Thanks, although now I'm a self-employed, professional, computer geek."

"Excellent. I would like to engage your services."

"What do you need?"

"Well, it's kind of a long story."

"It always is with you. Give me the IMDb version."

"Well, I'm currently working as a Managing Agent for a realty company and one of the tenants in my building has disappeared."

"Okay. Do they owe a lot of back rent?"

"He did, but at the time he seemed to have disappeared, he didn't."

"I don't get it," says Tank.

"He had everything on autopay with his bank. It looks like he disappeared before the money ran out, so we didn't start seeing arrears until after he was gone. By then, the Covid restrictions were in place, so we couldn't go to court to reclaim the space. When a judge was finally able to rule on it, the tenant had been reported to the NYPD as a missing person."

"Do they have any leads on him?" asks Tank.

"Nope. It looks like they just put it into the circular file. Anyway, the reason I'm reaching out to you is that I managed to get hold of a computer he left behind in the apartment. I was wondering if you'd be able to go into it and do some digging around? You know, find out passwords and stuff so we can see what his internet activity was."

After a pause, Tank replies, "You do know that's called hacking and it's illegal if it's not being done by law enforcement."

"How about this," replies Marsh, "according to real estate law, anything left behind in an apartment by a tenant must be put in storage for 30 days. After that, if it isn't claimed by the tenant or a relative, it's public property for whoever wants it. This dude has no kin to claim anything and the 30-day period on his computer will be ending this week. After it does, yours truly will be the new owner."

"Okay, contact me then and I can probably do it. What type of machine is it?"

"A Mac Power Book."

"Do you know how old it is?"

"Nope."

"Okay, whatever. Bring it in and I'll take a look."

"How about next weekend?"

"Sure, bring it around late in the afternoon next Saturday."

"Cool. Where?"

"I'll text you my shop's address."

"Your shop? I guess that means I now have my own cyber-security expert."

"Yeah, and now I know a landlord. If you have any cheap apartment listings, bring those with you too."

"No problem. What are you in the market for?" asks Marsh, "open concept, ensuite bathroom, central air, condo, co-op? We'll talk next weekend."

"You got it. By the way, I understood everything you just said. I watch HGTV every week with my lady."

"So do I....Whoops!"

"Fuck off," laughs Tank, and hangs up.

25

Every time Marsh saw Tank, he couldn't help but feel a brotherly connection. After all, he was the one who originally gave this hulking Jewish kid named Eben Moskowitz his nickname. Even though on the surface it would seem that "Tank" referred to his friend's size, it turned out that Marsh gave him the handle because big Eben's prowess at video games reminded him of the tech-savvy character that piloted the Nebuchadnezzar in the Matrix movie.

When Marsh got out of the elevator and followed the signs to suite 231, he was amused (but not surprised) to find a sign that read "Matrix Solutions" on the door.

Once he was buzzed into the office, Marsh found his old friend pretty much as he remembered him; solid and intense-looking, but with kind eyes and a mischievous smile.

"Look at you," says Marsh, "with your big old office in a midtown high-rise. I wouldn't be surprised if you had the Key Maker and the Oracle working in the back."

"Good to see you buddy," says Tank. "Unfortunately, I'm the only one in today. I gave the Key Maker and the Oracle the day off."

"Seriously, dude, how many people do you have working for you?"

"I have a partner and a few employees."

"A partner? Anybody I know?"

"Nah, somebody I met in Grad School."

"So, it's just going to be you and me here to do this." says Marsh, taking a sweeping look around the reception area.

"Yeah, it shouldn't take too long and then we'll do happy hour. There's a place nearby on Third Avenue I like to visit sometimes after work."

"What's it called?" asks Marsh, looking back at his friend.

"Hudson Malone."

Marsh smiles. "Don't know it, but I'm game.

"Don't worry, you'll love it. So, let's see what you brought me."

Marsh removes a shiny silver laptop from his shoulder bag and hands it over to Tank.

"Follow me," instructs Tank, as he leads Marsh down a corridor and into a well-lit, spacious room with several individual workstations. After Tank takes a seat and instructs Marsh to pull up a chair, he starts to hook up the necessary cables for the process of entering someone else's cyber-world.

"How does this all work?" asks Marsh.

As he continues hooking up the laptop, Tank replies, "First, I'm going to boot the computer into a different operating system to bypass the login screen. Then I'll get into the drive and start browsing the passwords. After that, I'll go into his internet history. That'll take a minute, but eventually we'll be able to see all the sites this person went to on the web."

"Cool," replies Marsh as he watches his friend work.

26

"Most of the places your guy Doug went on the internet are pretty standard," says Tank. "Amazon, Spotify, YouTube, etc. It doesn't seem like he was too interested in social media though. He has some profiles, but there's really no info on them and he has very few contacts. On the other hand, there is a lot of chat site activity. Not odd for the pandemic. A lot of folks were looking for anonymous companionship in cyberspace. Most of the hookup sites he trafficked are also pretty common, except this one."

"What's that?" asks Marsh.

"ChatEntropy," replies Tank, as his voice trails off.

"Never heard of it," says Marsh.

"Yeah, it's a little esoteric. It was a trending video chat site for about a minute during the pandemic. It was kind of like Omegle or ChatRoulette from back in the day. You know, random encounters, sometimes raunchy, sometimes funny, and often very freaky. It was essentially populated by a lot of consenting adults who were against censorship of any kind."

"That could be a lead," says Marsh.

"If it's still around," says Tank. "By the way, it looks like this guy's username on the site was 'Nameless'.

"Anonymous handle for an anonymous site, muses Marsh, adding, "What do you mean if the site's still around?"

"Many of these random, freestyle sites had problems with complaints about their unregulated content. Stuff like hardcore porn, and in some cases, even kids. A lot of it came under law enforcement scrutiny and they either cleaned up, disappeared, or maybe even migrated onto the dark web. Although if ChatEntropy has migrated to the dark web, it won't be a video chat site anymore."

"Why?"

"For a video chat you'd have to grant access to your computer's camera. That would automatically reveal the IP address and kind of defeat the whole anonymity thing of the Dark Web. Plus, a lot more data is needed for video chat and the Dark Web is just too slow."

"So, what you're telling me is that searching for ChatEntropy on the Dark Web could end up being a big nothing burger?"

"Perhaps, but maybe being a video chat site isn't its front anymore? Maybe the video part only comes after you hook-up privately with a like-minded freak?

"Got it," says Marsh, adding, "I don't know about you, but I'd like to find out what happened to ChatEntropy."

"Moving forward with this would be against my better judgment, "replies Tank, "but that's been the case with a lot of the shit I've done with you."

27

As they sit over a couple of designer beers in Hudson Malone, Marsh continues asking questions about what they had been doing in Tank's studio.

"Is it common to have a site like ChatEntropy turn up in a search and then have none of the links work?"

"Yes, and no," replies Tank.

"What does it mean?"

"If a normal Google search isn't turning up anything current, then the site probably isn't putting up content on the commercial web anymore."

"Okay, then what?"

"Maybe it's defunct, or perhaps there actually is another version of it on the Dark Web."

"You mentioned that before," says Marsh, "but then you also said it wouldn't be a video chat site anymore. No, wait, you mentioned that contacts could be made on the Dark Web, but then the actual video site may be somewhere else."

Have you ever been on the Dark Web?" asks Tank.

"Nope, I've only heard of it. That's why I decided to get in touch with a computer genius like you."

"You don't need to be a computer genius to go on the dark web."

"Okay, but since I have absolutely no idea what the Dark Web actually is, do you think you can give me some pointers?"

"How about if I give you a warning first?" says Tank. "Then you can decide if you still want pointers."

"A warning?"

"Yeah. What do you know about the Dark Web?"

"Like I said, I've heard the name. That's about it."

"You haven't changed; still Mister leap-before-you-look."

"Hey, I haven't leaped anywhere yet. In fact, I've decided to consult an expert first," replies Marsh with a smug smile.

"Okay, then let's consult," says Tank. "The basic definition of the Dark Web is that it's a cyber environment for encrypted online content that's not indexed by conventional search engines. That means it's a place where folks who don't want to be found out can browse and/or do whatever they want online with total anonymity."

"If no one wants to be found out, then how does anyone find anything?"

"Not a bad question. There are search engines designed specifically for the Dark Web, like the Hidden Wiki, or DuckDuckGo. These kinds of browsers don't keep tabs on your searches and don't share your info. That way, you can find just about anything you want, legal or illegal without leaving a trace that you were there."

"Okay, how do I get on the Dark Web?"

"First, you need to download the Tor browser.

"Did you say Tor?"

"Yeah, it's an acronym for "The Onion Router." It's free to download for Mac, Android, and Linux systems."

"Does that mean all I need to do to get on the Dark Web is download this browser and then I can find a search engine and look for ChatEntropy?"

"Basically, but there's also some other stuff you need to keep in mind."

"Like what?" asks Marsh.

"Searching on the Dark Web isn't like browsing on the regular web. It's a lot sketchier. Most Dark Web search engines turn up addresses that are old, irrelevant, or repeat hits. That's because a lot of the stuff on the Dark Web is illegal and sites routinely change addresses to keep things fluid. There are also no simple Dark Web addresses, like Target.com. Dark Web URLs are usually insanely long and complex. The reason for that is when you search for something on the Dark Web you're not brought directly to what you're looking for. Instead, your search is directed through a series of random servers so that it becomes encrypted, and hence, untraceable. Because of that encryption process, searching for stuff on the Dark Web can end up being both time consuming and tedious."

After giving Marsh a moment to take it all in, Tank then adds, "Not to mention that much of what happens on the Dark Web is not only weird and sketchy, but illegal. If you're going to use it, make sure you're just looking and not buying anything. Don't ever tell anyone your real name or share any personal info."

"You're not exactly selling the experience," says Marsh dryly.

"Sorry for sounding like a dad," says Tank. "I just wanted you to be fully aware of the gravitas of the situation."

After a brief silence, Marsh assures him, "That's cool. I appreciate you laying it out like it is."

"I hope I'm not getting all up in your business by asking this," says Tank, "but why do you need to look for this person? Did you know him?"

"Nope, never met the dude."

"So then why are you acting like you're Philip Marlowe? What does this person mean to you?"

"I don't know if I can explain it. I just got this weird feeling while I was standing in the guy's apartment, and my boss told me he disappeared. How does somebody just disappear? I mean if this guy could just vanish into thin air, then you or I could disappear too, right? It's a complete mystery and I guess I'm intrigued by it."

"Do you really think you're going to find this guy?" asks Tank.

Marsh shrugs. "Probably not, but I feel like I have to try."

"It's not going to be easy," says Tank. "No one ever uses their real name on the Dark Web. We found his username this afternoon from when ChatEntropy was legit, but if it's on the Dark Web now then maybe he's changed his username? If that's the case, then he's going to be like a grain of sand on the beach. Do you understand?"

"I know what I'm hoping to do probably sounds naive and pointless," says Marsh. "Like being a teenager on mushrooms and thinking you can run closer to the sunset. But there's something else too. I'm not sure I can put it into words. The disappearance of this guy is speaking to some weird sense of inevitability and dread within me that I can't ignore or explain. All I can say is that I need to find out what happened to this dude because somehow, one way or another, the same thing is eventually going to happen to all of us and I want to get a handle on it."

"Are you saying you think he's dead? If that's the case, then why bother?"

"I don't know. Maybe that's precisely why I need to look?"

"You're not making sense, why do you need to look? And for what, if you think he's likely dead?"

Marsh glances down for a moment, but then quickly looks up and stares deeply into his friend's eyes.

"All I want to know is if you can help me?"

"What exactly is it you want?" says Tank.

"Show me how to get on the Dark Web. Show me how to download Tor, navigate my way around."

"It's risky."

"I know."

"Maybe you do, maybe you don't. On the other hand, I have some additional considerations to think of. I'm a legit tech businessman now and I have a lot to lose if I accidently get into some shady shit on the Dark Web. Once there was a time, but now the Feds are always prowling around out there and I'm over messing around with that kind of stuff."

Marsh suddenly becomes very serious. "I totally understand dude, and I would never expect you to risk your livelihood. Just get me started and I'll take my chances."

Both men are silent for a few seconds when Tank asks, "What do you intend to do with the guy's computer?"

Looking down at the computer next to him in the booth, Marsh replies, "I haven't really thought about it."

"The reason I'm asking is because if you want to go on the Dark Web, I can wipe his machine clean and you can use that."

"I don't know how I'd feel about erasing what's left of his life," says Marsh.

"I could put anything important on a USB," says Tank. It's up to you. But I would suggest that if you're going on the Dark Web, you shouldn't use your own computer."

"Why?"

"Because if you accidentally slip up and your machine gets breached, you could lose your whole life, if you know what I mean. If you don't want me to wipe his computer for you, then buy yourself a cheap pc to go on the Dark Web."

For a few moments, Marsh sits there in deep thought. "You're right," he finally says to his friend. "This guy doesn't seem to have left anyone behind, so I guess whatever personal stuff is on his computer doesn't matter anymore."

"It's up to you," says Tank," but what else are you going to do, throw his computer out? If you do that, his data is going to be lost forever anyway."

"If you're willing to wipe the computer clean for me, does that mean you'll also help me get on the Dark Web?" asks Marsh with a sly smile.

After a long pause, Tank reluctantly replies, "Sure, I'll help you lose your law-abiding virginity."

28

The following weekend, Marsh returned to Tank's studio on a Saturday afternoon to pick up the recently-wiped computer and get started on the Dark Web.

"In case you ever need them, I saved all his files on a thumb drive," says Tank. "You never know what you might find and maybe they'll be helpful."

"Thanks," says Marsh, taking the thumb drive from his friend."

"So, are you ready to get started?

"Sure," says Marsh, "let's get this show on the road."

After Tank fires up the newly scrubbed computer, he angles it around so he can start showing his friend what to do.

"We're going to begin by heading to the Tor project website so we can download the browser for free."

As Tank works the keyboard, Marsh watches while images of his friend's namesake from the Matrix comes to mind.

"Looks good so far," says Tank. "I just downloaded the version for Mac OS, no problem. Next, I'm going to install GPGTools so we can verify the program signature."

"What does that mean?" asks Marsh.

"It's to ensure you're getting an official version of Tor and not some hacker's knock-off. That's why we have to confirm the document signature with Tor. Once the download is complete, I'll open the .dmg file and then we can start installing it.

While Marsh sits and watches his friend work, he begins to wonder what he's going to do if he actually *does* find Doug Morrison on the Dark Web.

29

"Here you go," says Tank, as both he and Marsh look at what's on the screen in front of them. "Welcome to the Dark Web."

"It looks like a regular search page," replies Marsh.

"It is. I just opted for this one because I think some of the others have certain bugs in them that can be concerning. To give you an appetizer, I'm gonna do a search here for 'The Darknet Black Market'." After he taps in the search, a list of sites eventually appears.

"Lo and behold, look what comes up first," says Tank, "a site with that exact name. Let's see what's on it."

After clicking the link and waiting again, the site eventually comes up. "Are those credit cards?" asks Marsh, looking at rows of Visa cards on the screen with various dollar amounts entered under each one.

"Yes, they are," says Tank. "Those are some poor, unfortunate people's credit card numbers, which are now for sale to whoever would like to try and commit credit card fraud."

"Let me see this," says Marsh, as he leans in closer to the screen. "It says that the max for this card is $10,000, and you can buy it for $55. Is this stuff real?"

"Maybe yes, maybe no. Like I've been trying to tell you, the dark web is a lawless place."

"So let me get this straight. By trying to buy one of these cards to rip off a stranger, you could possibly end up getting ripped off yourself by the site you're buying from.

"That's correct."

"I'm certainly not interested in that kind of crap. Who would be?"

"Criminals," says Tank matter-of-factly. "That's what the Black Market is, illegal items being sold between people breaking the law."

"I get it," remarks Marsh. "Can we look at some chat sites instead?"

"Of course," says Tank as he enters in a new search. "I didn't think you were interested in bogus credit cards for sale. I just wanted to let you see what's up. But just so you know, there's a lot more fucked up stuff than that for sale on the Dark Web, so be careful of who you interact with, as well as what you click on."

After keying in another search, Tank gets them on a group chat site and then turns the computer around so Marsh can access the keyboard. "Pick a username," he says.

As Marsh tries to think of an appropriate handle, Tank adds, "I have us on a group chat. That way, it'll probably be easier to get a response if you throw your question into a crowd instead of slogging through a lot of individual chats."

"Makes sense," says Marsh. A moment later he smiles, looks at Tank, and then starts typing. When he's done, he turns the computer around so Tank can see what was typed.

"Seraph," announces Tank, and then smiles. "Nice. The name of The Oracle's bodyguard from the Matrix."

"I thought you'd like that."

"I do, I do."

"Now what?" asks Marsh.

"Start typing and tell the people what you want."

"Okay," replies Marsh, as he starts to recite aloud what he's typing.

"Does anyone out there know about ChatEntropy?"

A few seconds later someone named piedpiper333 types back. *"What r u looking 4?"*

"A *chat site called ChatEntropy?"*

"What kind of site?"

Marsh looks at Tank, who responds with a shrug.

"A hook-up site, I think," says Marsh aloud as he types.

"Are you interested in chics or dicks?" types piedpiper333.

"I'm interested in the site ChatEntropy. Have u ever heard of it?"

"No."

"Do you know anyone who has?"

Someone else with the handle Wacdaddy enters the chat and types, *"I'm looking 4 a jerk, any 1 interested?*

"I think the first dude has probably split," says Tank, looking over his friend's shoulder.

Marsh asks Wacdaddy, *"Hey have u ever heard of a site called ChatEntropy?"*

"Are u a jerk?" asks Wacdaddy.

"No, do you know anything about ChatEntropy?"

When there's no response, Marsh says to Tank, "I can see how this could get very tedious."

"I don't want to sound like a broken record," says Tank, "but welcome to the Dark Web."

Following another few encounters that answer his questions with vague, secretive, and even stupid responses, Marsh goes back to the browser and begins looking for some other sites.

“I have to take care of a few things,” says Tank. “If you need any help, just give me a shout.”

Marsh nods in response and then dives headlong into his search until Tank eventually returns a while later and tells him he’s closing shop so they can go have happy hour at Hudson Malone’s.

30

As the bartender delivers their first round, Tank looks up and down the bar before swooping in like a hawk and asking Marsh, "Now that you've been on the Dark Web, what do you think your chances are of finding this dude, what's his name again?"

"Doug, but his last known handle is Nameless."

"Right, so what do you think your chances are of finding Nameless?"

"A lot slimmer than I thought if I have to keep texting with monosyllabic deviants."

Tank laughs. "The Dark Web is designed for anonymity. People who use it generally don't want to be found. They just want to indulge whatever they're into and keep it on the downlow. That doesn't mean you won't ever come across somebody that can tell you something about ChatEntropy, but since everybody's using an alias on the Dark Web, you'll probably never find this guy Nameless."

"I'm aware of that," replies Marsh, as he takes a drink of his beer.

"Then why bother?" asks Tank.

"Because believe it or not, it still seems like a good idea."

"It does?"

I'll admit that after today it looks highly unlikely that any of these disembodied voices in cyberspace will be able to tell me anything useful, but the journey itself still has a certain fascination."

"Like one more drink after you're already drunk?"

"In a way, but don't forget we're talking about someone's life here. A real person disappeared."

"Just be careful that what you're deciding to do doesn't end up doing you," warns Tank.

"I'll remember that, and if I ever find ChatEntropy, I'll send you a link."

The friends spoke no more that afternoon about either the Dark Web or Nameless, instead, they drank like you're supposed to at happy hour when you're with an old friend and all you're really looking for is a break from the world.

PART III

31

Much to his surprise, Marsh quickly becomes obsessed with searching around on the Dark Web. Even though he's aware that much of what he's encountering is either dangerous or crazy, he is nevertheless attracted to the otherworldliness of it all. Like the first time a kid from the suburbs goes into the hood to buy drugs and thinks the ghetto is somehow a cool and exotic place, that is, until something goes wrong.

On another level, Marsh also looks at his forays onto the Dark Web as a welcome escape from the passive-aggressive abuse he has been experiencing from Sal at work. The man is a control freak who depends on Marsh to do everything, yet at the same time he also goes out of his way to treat him like an idiot man-child.

At first, Marsh thought that being given the responsibility of prepping Doug Morrison's old apartment for the rental market would give him a certain autonomy with his boss. Yet what resulted turned out to be exactly the opposite. Sal is now up his ass non-stop from morning until night, five days a week. He even tried to haunt Marsh over the weekend, but Marsh was smart enough not to answer the phone that first Saturday morning when he recognized the number. The following Monday he simply lied and told Sal that he usually went out of town on the weekends.

It had been a little more than a month now since Tank had set him up with Doug Morrison's old computer, and for the better part of at least one day each weekend Marsh would do a deep dive into the Dark Web to search for the notorious ChatEntropy.

During that time, he chatted on a myriad of sites with every type of internet weirdo imaginable as they foraged around for all kinds of shit. From illicit sex and drugs, to weapons, cryptocurrency, financial fraud, murder for hire, child pornography, and even deprogrammers for extraterrestrial abductees. He had heard it all.

On this rainy Saturday night, Marsh, a.k.a. Seraph, is halfway through a six pack of his favorite craft beer when he enters what will be his fourth (or perhaps fifth?) chat site that evening.

32

Seraph: *Is there anybody out there?*

Sarathi1334: *I am*

Seraph: *How r u?*

Sarathi1334: *I am*

Seraph: *Ok. Can I ask u something?*

Sarathi1334: *Yes*

Seraph: *Do u know anything about a site called ChatEntropy?*

Sarathi1334: *Why?*

Seraph: *It disappeared from the regular internet, and I want to reconnect if it's on the Dark Web*

Sarathi1334: *What r u looking for?*

Seraph: *A guy*

Sarathi1334: *For what?*

Seraph: *He disappeared, and I want to find him*

Sarathi1334: *Does he want to be found?*

Seraph: *I'd like to hear that from him*

Sarathi1334: *What is he called?*

Seraph: *Nameless*

When Sarathi1334 doesn't respond, Marsh suspects he's been ghosted and decides to wait and see if anyone else shows up. It doesn't take long before another handle eventually comes up on the screen.

Krishna11: *Is Seraph here?*

Seraph: *Yes. Who r u?*

Krishna11: *I can take u where u want to go*

Seraph: *Where is that?*

Krishna11: *2 the nameless 1*

Seraph: *On this site?*

Krishna11: *No, another*

Seraph: *On the dark web?*

Krishna11: *No, another place*

Seraph: *Where?*

When Krishna11 doesn't immediately respond, Marsh starts to think that maybe he's encountered yet another Dark Web trickster just having fun.

After waiting a minute or so, Marsh decides to give it another try before moving on.

Seraph: *Krishna 11 r u still there?*

Krishna11: *R u ready?*

Seraph: *4 what?*

Krishna11: *4 all*

Seraph: *What does that mean?*

Krishna11: *Nothing 0*

Seraph: *What?*

Krishna11: *Everything 1*

Seraph: *I don't understand*

Krishna11:
01010101010101010101010101010101010101010101.......

Seraph: ?

Once again, what seems like a long time passes without a response from Krishna 11.

Seraph: *Krishna11 if that's all, I have 2 go*

Krishna11: *Go here...*

Krishna11:
*tor66/search?q=chatentrop&aqs=y/69i369j14285714285714285714285714285714285714285714285714285714285714285714285714285714285*7142857<>^v.onion

Seraph: *Is this the address for ChatEntropy?*

Krishna11: *It's where u need 2 go*

Seraph: *What do you mean? Is this the address for ChatEntropy or not?*

When there's no response, a sinking feeling causes Marsh to suspect that Krishnan is gone for good, yet he continues to wait anyway.

After a minute, Marsh tries again, but when it's obvious their conversation is over, he simply sits there with his beer and stares uneasily at what he's just been told is the address for exactly what he's been looking for.

33

"Be careful what you ask for, you just might get it," Marsh whispers to himself, as he hovers the cursor over the link Krishnan has left for him.

He is certainly familiar enough with the workings of the Dark Web to not worry about visiting another site, but no matter how many times he keeps reminding himself of that, there's still something holding Marsh back from clicking on the link.

After telling himself he'll take one more swig of beer and then do it, Marsh discovers that the can of beer next to him is empty.

"What's your problem?" he says out loud in his frustration. "You've been working on your own time for over a month to get to this point and this is your first lead, so what the hell are you waiting for?"

When his annoyance finally tips the scales away from his hesitancy, Marsh clicks the link and anxiously waits for what's next.

34

The homepage of ChatEntropy is surprisingly non-descript. All that's there is the word "ChatEntropy" in a large, stylized font and "Enter" in a smaller typeface underneath.

When he clicks "Enter," Marsh is presented with a pop-up box that asks him to type in a username.

After he types in the nickname "Seraph" and hits return, a new screen opens with a live video feed featuring an indigenous looking young man with straight, jet-black hair tied in a small bun at the top of his head. With full lips, an aristocratically curved nose, and deep, dark eyes like black olives, this young man looks like a character right out of a Mayan codex. Yet what is truly striking about his appearance, is that half of the young man's face is tattooed to look like a skeleton.

As Marsh takes in this exotic and somewhat ghoulish looking face staring back at him, he eyes divert momentarily to notice a green button in the lower right corner of the screen marked "Next."

Looking back again at the face on the screen, Marsh solemnly says, "hi," and manages to squeeze out a polite smile.

The man responds with a grim, silent nod of his head.

"Do you visit this site often?" asks Marsh.

Without blinking, the man responds, "Má tin naátik."

Not understanding what the young man just said, yet also not knowing what else to do, Marsh automatically continues in English. "I was wondering if I could ask you a question?"

Maintaining the blank, depthless stare of a lizard, the young man grimly shakes his head 'no' and then unceremoniously disappears and leaves Marsh looking at a blank screen.

35

After hitting "Next," Marsh finds himself confronted by another man. This time it's a rather Aryan looking dude with a tightly drawn, bony face that appears neither old nor young. He has very short, bleached hair, icy blue eyes, and a strange skin texture that catches the light as if it's made of white velvet.

He initially stares at Marsh with a very creepy half-smile and then asks through perfect white teeth, "You seem lost my friend, how can I help?"

"I'm not lost, but I'm looking for someone who might be."

"Of course. Tell me everything."

"I'm looking for someone that calls himself Nameless. Have you ever come across anyone with that username?"

"Who are you to him?" asks the man.

"Nobody special. I just need to find him."

"Nobody to a nameless person, sounds like you're looking for the answer to a riddle.

"Are you the sort of person who can help me answer riddles?"

"Perhaps. Here's one for you to think about. What is the most hazardous place in the universe?"

"Let me guess," says Marsh, trying to project a sense of levity, "this site, and I should go back to where I've come from?"

"Oh no," replies the man, who then emphasizes, "*I* is the most hazardous place in the universe."

"You may be right," says Marsh uncomfortably.

"I know I am. Would you like me to show you?"

"Maybe later," says Marsh, "but for now you'll have to excuse me." He then quickly hits 'Next' and exits.

36

Marsh's next chat buddy is an old black woman in a wheelchair. He knows this because the screen of her computer is tilted slightly toward the floor so he can see the curved tops of the chair's wheels.

The woman's head appears round and sturdy under a graying and nappy head of hair, while her aged, yellowing skin seems to drape on her like a dusty carpet.

Like his previous chat encounter, this woman also has a certain coldness in her eyes as she seems to be curled in her wheelchair like a cobra who is trying to hypnotize her prey.

"Hello there young man," she says, in a crude sounding voice that holds an echo of some past debauchery in it.

"Hello," replies Marsh, playing the polite young man he was raised to be.

"What brings you to this remote place," says the woman.

"I'm trying to find someone."

"A sweetheart?" she asks.

"No, a friend that I think is somewhere on this site."

"What makes you think that? Why would they be in this place."

"I don't know. I'm only here because someone gave me the link."

"What's your name?" asks the woman.

"Seraph."

"Oh, that's not a real name. That's just a nickname to hide behind. My name is Roberta Elder, what's yours?"

"The person I'm looking for is called Nameless, does that ring a bell?"

"Tell me your name and I'll try to remember."

"I already have," says Marsh. "Maybe I should go."

"What's your rush? I can show you a place where you can make lots of money. I even know where you can meet women, if you know what I mean.” Her face now suddenly takes on a lascivious and sadistic expression. “Just tell me your name,” she says, smiling like a hyena.

“Maybe another time,” says Marsh, as he clicks the 'Next' button.

37

The next individual Marsh finds himself looking at is a middle-aged, professorial looking type. He's wearing round, black rimmed spectacles, and his lumpy face looks like it's being strangled by the collar of his stiff white shirt and tightly-knotted necktie.

From what appears to be an office, he sits there staring blankly at Marsh. Then, without warning, his mouth slowly stretches into a thin, brittle grin.

"Hello," he says in a soft Scottish accent, "my name is Doctor Cameron."

"My name is Seraph."

"An angelic name," he says, with a reverent lilt in his voice. "Are you a person of faith?"

"Not particularly," replies Marsh.

"That's okay. We should only have faith in what we know."

When Marsh nods in agreement, Cameron quietly announces, “If you don’t mind, I’d like to shed a little light on the subject.”

Before Marsh can respond, the lighting in Dr. Cameron’s space suddenly changes from that of a normal office or home into complete darkness. A second later, the darkness is unexpectedly pierced by a rapidly flashing strobe light accompanied by a steady, dull thumping sound.

“Just look through the light and keep your eyes on me,” says the Doctor in his thin Scottish brogue. “Let my voice be your anchor if you’re feeling adrift.

As Marsh looks on, the Doctor continues to repeat slowly, “let my voice be your anchor if you’re feeling adrift. Let my voice be your anchor if you’re feeling adrift.”

Let my voice be your anchor if you’re feeling adrift.

Without being consciously aware of the strobe light and pulsing noise ever stopping, Marsh suddenly finds himself once again sitting quietly in his apartment and looking at the computer screen. Except now the person looking back at him is not Doctor Cameron.

The face on the screen is too blurry for Marsh to make out, but the seemingly bald head, pale skin, and deep watery eyes of this person reminds him of Gollum from the *Lord of the Rings* movie. As he tries to get a clearer look at who this dude is, Marsh can't help but notice that the black pullover sweater he's wearing seems to be pulsing with a life of its own.

"Hello?" says Marsh to the person on the screen. "Can you hear me?"

Whoever it is gives no indication that they can hear anything, yet in the following instant a deep, heavily distorted voice erupts from the computer and slowly responds with what sounds like, "What... do... you.... want?"

"I'm sorry," says Marsh, "but are you asking what I want?"

While the man on the screen remains motionless and unresponsive, a faint electronic hum begins that quickly starts to get louder and louder.

While this is going on, Marsh notices that the image on screen is also beginning to come more sharply into focus.

Just as the hum from the computer hits a deafening crescendo, Marsh suddenly sees that what he thought was a black pullover worn by this Gollum look-a-like is actually a swarm of live, winged insects covering his arms and torso.

As Marsh recoils in surprise, the screen suddenly goes dark. When the image returns an instant later, Gollum is still there, although this time he's wearing an actual black sweater.

"Hello," he says, smiling benevolently. "How can I help?"

Now that Marsh can see him more clearly, he realizes that this person really doesn't look like Gollum at all, despite being pale and hairless. Marsh also notices that his eyes are uncharacteristically dark for someone of such a light complexion. In fact, the closer he looks, the harder it is for Marsh to see any white at all in this man's eyes.

As Marsh silently processes all this, the pale man on the screen continues talking.

"I've never seen you before," he says. "Is this your first time here?"

When Marsh fails to respond, the man keeps going.

"We don't get all that many visitors here. What were you looking for that brought you to this place?"

"A site called ChatEntropy," replies Marsh, with a hesitancy and unsteadiness that surprises him.

"Well, you've made it, but what exactly did you think you would find here?"

"I'm looking for a friend," says Marsh, still feeling somewhat unsure of himself, as if he were rediscovering how to talk.

"Does this friend have a name?" asks the man.

After taking a good long look at the man's sweater to make sure it's no longer made of live insects, Marsh quietly replies, "Nameless."

The man appears surprised at Marsh's answer, followed by his image once again going out of focus and his shirt once more taking on a pulsating life of its own.

Marsh can only sit and watch as the entire image on the screen slowly turns into a blurry, amorphous blob and the distorted, electronic voice he had heard

earlier returns to slowly warn him,
"Be...Care.....Full.

38

After coming back from what feels like a deep sleep, Marsh discovers he's once again sitting at his computer and staring at the ChatEntropy home screen.

It takes a moment for him to get his bearings, but once he does, he turns and starts to look around at the inside of his apartment to verify that he's not dreaming, or hallucinating, or losing his fucking mind.

"What the hell just happened," he thinks, as he leans back in his chair and stares blankly at the 'Next' button in the lower right-hand corner of the computer screen.

The more he tries to think, the more Marsh feels like he's hungover, not from alcohol, but rather from a vast blankness of both thought and feeling.

He looks again at the 'Next' button on the computer, yet the thought of pushing it and thrusting himself back into Chatentropy makes him suddenly feel like one of those stupid characters in a horror movie that are always choosing to go toward the danger, while everyone in the theatre is yelling at the screen, "Don't do it!"

After spacing out a little while longer, Marsh finally decides to log out of Tor and go to bed. Maybe a good night's sleep will help him process some of the unexplainable weirdness he's just experienced.

PART IV

39

With a new work week in front of him, Marsh feels relieved at being able to turn away from ChatEntropy and once again fully immerse himself in the responsibilities of his daily life. For one thing, he had been too caught up in his online exploits to celebrate, or even acknowledge, that Doug Morrison's apartment finally had a new tenant. It had been sitting on the market for longer than expected, which of course got Marsh some cynical remarks from Sal, as if he somehow hadn't done a good job supervising the renovation.

"Fuck that asshole," Marsh thinks to himself as he gets ready to leave his apartment, "I'm not sure how much longer I can put up with his bullshit."

Even though he knew what was waiting for him, Marsh was nonetheless hoping that getting up, going to work, and the monotony of his commute would all end up being welcome distractions after the weirdness he had encountered that past weekend on ChatEntropy. For example, the guy wearing the shirt made of living insects. Who could ever find a place in their head where that would fit?

Yet even while he continued to talk himself into the virtues of avoiding ChatEntropy and its weirdness, for the rest of that week Marsh still found himself waking up every morning at the tail end of a dream about the site.

When the work week is eventually over and 5pm on Friday finally rolls around like the Mister Softee truck on a hot summer day, rather than going back onto the dark web as he'd planned, Marsh instead decides to have a mental health evening and postpone his Chatentropy adventures until Saturday. After picking up some beer and takeout, he makes a firm decision while heading home that this is going to be an evening of cold beers, relaxed brainwaves, an escapist movie, and nothing else.

40

On Saturday, rather than immediately returning to the Dark Web, Marsh instead gets a hunch that he should do a Google search on his own computer for the doctor he had encountered on ChatEntropy.

It takes him a few moments, but eventually Marsh remembers his name was Cameron.

After checking out a few hits, he finally comes across an entry for a Doctor Donald Ewen Cameron. Recognizing the picture in the profile as the man he spoke to on ChatEntropy, Marsh starts to read about how Doctor Cameron was one of the main psychiatrists involved in the notorious MK Ultra project in the 1960's.

Run by the CIA, MK Ultra was the code name for a long-term series of mind control experiments in which the good Doctor and others like him used substances like LSD, the paralytic drug curare, and electroconvulsive therapy to control and manipulate subjects. The specific protocol Cameron invented was a technique known as 'psychic driving', which consisted of putting a subject into a drug induced coma for as long as 30 days while playing tape loops of noise and repetitive commands.

"My God!" thinks Marsh, "this guy was a fucking monster."

As he continues reading, Marsh also comes across another surprising little tidbit. It turns out that Doctor Cameron died in 1965.

"What the hell," says Marsh to himself aloud. "If he died almost 60 years ago, how on earth was I able to talk with him on ChatEntropy last weekend? That's just fucking nuts!"

It certainly was, but it also made Marsh realize that maybe he should start taking his misgivings about the site a little more seriously. The things he's been seeing and hearing are not just simply weird and disorienting, ChatEntropy also seems to be affecting his overall state of mind regarding reality in general.

He also remembered the black woman he had talked to just before he met the Doctor. The one in the wheelchair.

"I wonder who she is?" he thinks. "What if she's also dead?"

For the next little while, Marsh sits back, nurses his coffee, and wracks his brain to try and remember what that woman's name was.

41

When his efforts at trying to remember the old black woman's name fail to produce an *aha!* moment, Marsh finishes his coffee and deposits the cup in the kitchen sink. On his way back to the computer, he decides to grab his phone and walks over to the window to take a break. After a few moments of looking down at the street, Marsh unlocks his phone and starts to check his Google feed.

The first item he comes across is an ad for one of those cheesy internet articles about the 10 most gruesome Black Serial Killers.

"What's this?" he thinks, mildly amused. "There were actually black serial killers? I always thought that was a white thing." Curious, he opens the article and scrolls down to see what it's about. The first name Marsh comes across is that of a woman named Roberta Elder, formally known as 'Atlanta's Mrs. Bluebeard'.

"Holy shit," he says to himself, after looking at the old photograph of her. "That's the woman I saw on ChatEntropy."

As he reads on, Marsh comes to discover that Mrs. Elder had poisoned to death at least 14 different people, some of whom were family members that had life insurance policies with her named as a beneficiary. It also said she was given a life sentence in 1952 at the age of 43, and that she likely died behind bars.

"Likely died behind bars," Marsh thinks to himself. "That was over 70 years ago. That means the woman I talked with on ChatEntropy is over 110 years old."

42

As Marsh puts down his phone and gazes out the window into the street below, he tries to figure if there would be any advantages to searching again on ChatEntropy for either Doctor Cameron or Mrs. Elder?

The possibility of talking to a pair of dead people again would certainly be wild! Yet since his initial conversations with them were each kind of threatening, Marsh wonders if it is wise to put himself in harm's way again? After all, talking with Cameron resulted in his having some sort of psychotic break, and Mrs. Elder was/is a serial killer.

Marsh also couldn't figure out what either of these dead ghouls had to do with Doug Morrison? If he were to pursue their company, would he end up experiencing the same fate that Morrison had? Whatever that was? As he continues thinking, Marsh starts to wonder, not just about Morrison's disappearance in general, but specifically how he might have been assisted by some freak on ChatEntropy. Did Doug Morrison encounter something or someone like a Doctor Cameron or a

Mrs. Elder, who then lured him into some unspeakable end?

Without any answers for the thoughts swirling around in his head, nor with any clear idea of what he is going to do next, Marsh shuts down his machine and proceeds to fire up Doug Morrison's old computer.

43

The first chat screen that opens for Marsh after gaining access to ChatEntropy reveals a small room containing only a basic wooden table and a straight back chair.

After observing this minimal scenario for what seems like a long time, Marsh's attention is suddenly drawn to a fly buzzing around this onscreen room. Eventually, the insect lands on what looks like the inner surface of Marsh's computer screen.

For several seconds, Marsh watches the underbelly of the small insect as it wanders aimlessly across the screen, finally stopping for a moment to methodically rub its two front legs together.

As Marsh continues watching, the fly lowers its head and begins to stare directly at him. At this point, the insect's features start to mysteriously enlarge on the screen, accompanied by a strange and barely audible hissing sound. After a few seconds of this, Marsh begins to feel strangely disoriented. Is the insect actually getting bigger or is he somehow being drawn into the eyes of this creature? Once the bugs's eyes have taken over the entire computer screen, Marsh next finds himself becoming engrossed in the reflection he can now see of himself in the dark glass. He had never looked at his own face more closely than he was trying to now in the shadowy and distorted image within the insects' eyes. The chance to possibly discover something new about himself in this dark tableau has Marsh completely occupied, when suddenly there is a deafening roar that's immediately followed by the screen going dark.

A moment later, a new chat screen unexpectedly appears, and this one shows a view of the same room, except now there's a cat sitting in profile on the chair and staring somewhere offscreen.

As Marsh watches the cat, the creature slowly turns toward him, opens its mouth in a wide yawn, and releases a swarm of flies that move toward Marsh like an expanding black cloud. Within seconds, his view of the room becomes completely obliterated by this mass of flies, after which the screen once again goes dark.

At this point, Marsh abruptly jumps up and begins pacing back and forth in front of the computer.

"What the fuck is going on here!" he half-screams, pointing angrily at the black screen. "The other day it was a guy covered with flies, now it's a cat that spits out flies."

Over the next few minutes, Marsh is torn as he grapples between throwing Doug Morrison's computer out the window or getting back on ChatEntropy to see how deep the rabbit hole goes.

As he continues pacing, a sudden knock at the door causes him to stop and look suspiciously toward the entrance of his apartment.

Not expecting anyone, and not accustomed to having surprise visitors, Marsh remains motionless until a second, more forceful knock breaks the silence.

Fetching the baseball bat he keeps beside the door; Marsh takes it in one hand while using the other to open the peephole and look out into the hall.

Seeing no one there, Marsh closes the peephole and remains perfectly still for perhaps 30 seconds as he tries to listen if anyone is outside.

When no noise is forthcoming, Marsh waits for a bit longer before quietly opening the door to the limit of the security chain and peering outside.

Seeing no one, he proceeds to undo the chain and open the door. As soon as he does, Marsh is suddenly forced to recoil as an immense fly buzzes in his face, circles around him, and then quickly flies off down the hallway.

"What's with the fucking flies?!" he growls, after swatting at the air in front of his face and then angrily slamming the door shut.

44

Following this totally bizarre experience with the fly, Marsh walks over to his desk and takes a seat. It now starts to dawn on him that maybe his initial approach to the Douglas Morrison situation might have been a bit naïve.

Up until now, all the strange things he's experienced have occurred exclusively on the Dark Web. The fact that this latest incident managed to bleed over into his real life now makes Marsh think it might be time to reassess the situation.

First, this weird shit he's been encountering as of late would be almost impossible to prove to anyone else. He's thought of telling Tank about some of it, but without evidence, something like this recent business with the flies would only make his friend think he was losing it or maybe taking magic mushrooms. And forget about the business of talking with dead people. Telling anyone that would certainly land him in an asylum!

In spite of a feeling he'd had since he was younger that he wasn't like everyone else, Marsh is now slowly coming to grips with the fact that while we all dream of having adventures and being special, the reality is that the vast majority of the civilized world (including him) would much rather live vicariously through safe escapes that are manufactured for us, like a movie, or a tourist vacation, or even just a night out at a bar. In short, Marsh is finding that he's seriously considering that maybe he's had enough of ChatEntropy and whatever mysterious secrets he thought it might hold.

"What happened to Doug Morrison is between him and God," thinks Marsh. He's gone. To where, I don't know, and probably never will, but his apartment is rented, and my job is over. As he exits ChatEntropy, a fleeting thought suddenly crosses Marsh's mind that this could be the last time he'll ever see this site.

45

"Fate follows us all.
Destiny is how you choose
To struggle with it."

When Marsh finds this little haiku on a can of green tea he buys from a Japanese market, he can't help but feel a kind of foreboding.

Over the last couple of weeks, he'd felt okay about not being on ChatEntropy. Yet during this same period, he also began to feel like something was following him. Not anything tangible, like a person or an unpaid bill, instead it felt more like guilt. As if he should be doing something other than what he found himself doing on most days.

He tried to pretend that he didn't know what it was that made him feel like he was being followed, but deep down inside Marsh knew that ChatEntropy still had its hooks in him and there would be no peace until he dealt with it.

The chickens finally came home to roost regarding this feeling when Marsh couldn't sleep one night and tuned into Coast-to-Coast AM, a late-night, streaming talk show on all things paranormal.

That night's episode was on EVP (electronic voice phenomenon) a field originally pioneered by Ernst Senkowski and Konstantin Raudive in the 1970s. According to those who ascribe to EVP, there is a whole dimension of disincarnate entities that exist in the electro-magnetic waves that are prevalent all around us. In other words, things like tape recorders, televisions, and computers could all be potential portals to alternate realities and forms of existence.

Even though the show is interesting, Marsh nevertheless ends up falling asleep before it's over. It is sometime near dawn when he's unexpectedly awakened by the sound of static coming from his cellphone. While he lays there half-asleep, trying to get up the energy to reach over to the nightstand and turn the phone off, Marsh suddenly hears a voice from somewhere within the static say what sounds like, "Name…less."

Lifting his head and staring in sleepy disbelief at the phone, the static suddenly stops as abruptly as it started.

After examining his cell, Marsh now finds himself wide awake and thinking about whether or not what he just heard was real, as well as its possible ties to ChatEntropy.

46

The next day, as Marsh arrives home from work and opens the front door of his flat, his phone pings with an incoming message.

Dreading another neurotic, demanding communication from Sal, he goes about making himself comfortable before checking to see who it is.

He's surprised to see the text is from Tank, and all it includes is a link. Clicking on it, Marsh is eventually presented with what looks like an invoice. Under the listing of services provided are all the things that Tank had done to Doug Morrison's computer. Under the list of charges, it simply says, "Your company is required on Zoom tonight for a quick drink and catch up. Beneath that is a link for the meeting.

"I wonder what's on his mind," Marsh says to himself, while heading to the fridge for a beer.

A few minutes later Marsh logs into his Zoom meeting with Tank.

"Good evening, sir," says Marsh, as he removes the cap from his bottle of designer beer.

"How's the apprentice hacker?" asks Tank.

"It's all shits and giggles. I found this rad credit card site where like 80% of the numbers have paid off."

"Does that mean I can send you a real bill?" asks Tank.

"Not yet," replies Marsh sarcastically. "My subscribers are all late on their payments."

The two friends go on with their banter for another couple of minutes before Tank finally gets to what's on his mind.

"How's your search going?" he asks. "Have you found anything?"

"That would be an understatement," replies Marsh cryptically.

"I warned you about the Dark Web," says Tank.

"The Dark Web was fine. If you're not stupid, it's pretty obvious. ChatEntropy though, is something else entirely."

"You found it?"

"It would be more accurate to say it found me."

"Really? What was it like?"

"It's still a video platform."

"Holy shit, did you make yourself visible on the Dark Web?"

"I don't think so.....No."

"What do you mean? If you can be seen, then your IP address is vulnerable. Fuck, I warned you about that."

"It isn't what you think," mutters Marsh, realizing it's going to be harder to talk about this than he expected.

"Dude, if you can be seen by another person on the Dark Web, you're vulnerable. Period."

"I think Chatentropy is somewhere different than the rest of the Dark Web."

"What does that even mean?"

"I can't explain it," says Marsh, feeling like he did when his father caught him smoking weed when he was 15.

"What happened?" asks Tank in a flat, non-judgmental voice. "This is serious, talk to me."

The thought of trying to explain something like the guy with the insect shirt to his oldest friend starts to make Marsh feel very anxious.

As Tank continues to try and have a dialogue with him, Marsh begins to feel overwhelmed. The voice in his head keeps whispering over and over, "You spoke to dead people, dead serial killers, you can't tell anyone that." While Tank keeps asking him questions, Marsh continues to feel more and more like he'd rather disappear than have his friend think he's having a nervous breakdown. He also starts to suspect that maybe this is why Doug Morrison disappeared in the first place. How can he ever tell anyone about Doctor Cameron, Mrs. Elder, or the fucking flies without sounding like he's completely lost it?

For a moment, Marsh thinks that rather than trying to explain what he encountered on ChatEntropy, maybe he should just share the link with Tank?

No sooner does he think this, when the lights in his apartment start to noticeably flicker.

"What's going on there?" asks Tank, as he sees the lighting in Marsh's apartment dim.

"I don't know," says Marsh, looking quizzically at the flickering lights around him.

"Looks like a power surge," says Tank. After a moment, he adds, "You pay your Con ED bill?"

"Yes," replies Marsh. "I just think I'm tired," he says, changing the subject. "It's been a rough day and I probably don't know what I'm saying."

"About what?"

"I don't know."

As awkwardness and anxiety continue to crawl all over his body, it suddenly occurs to Marsh to lie.

"I didn't really go on ChatEntropy," he says, surprised at the sound of his own voice. "Some dude I encountered in one of the chat rooms told me ChatEntropy still existed as a video site on the Dark Web. I guess I believed him because I was frustrated and wanted to. I don't remember if he said he'd been on it, or if someone he knew had. I guess I believed him because he was the first person I've encountered so far who's said they've actually been on ChatEntropy."

"I don't know man," says Tank. "You should rethink continuing with this. It sounds like you're getting pretty stressed over it."

"Yeah," replies Marsh, seemingly agreeing with Tank, but also feeling relieved that he managed to dodge a bullet by lying. "After all, Doug Morrison's apartment has a new tenant so maybe I need to move on too."

"How come you didn't tell me that?" asks Tank.

"Does it really matter? He's still missing."

"Yeah, he is," replies his friend. "But you tried."

After a silent nod to conceal the anxiety he is actually feeling, Marsh lets his buddy slowly steer the conversation into a collage of snapshots from down memory lane, as the two friends begin to reminisce about the follies of their youth and the forgotten people from that period.

When they each eventually do a bottoms-up on their third beer, they agree to call it a night and promise to keep in touch.

47

Later that evening, Marsh is awakened by the sound of something moving around in the apartment.

Upon hearing it again, he sits up in bed and tries to focus on where the noise might be coming from.

From his position in the bedroom, Marsh can see most of the living room, as well as a portion of the kitchen. As he stares into the shadows, the movement of something running across the living room grabs his attention.

Startled, he moves quickly from the bed and proceeds cautiously toward the baseball bat that's by the front door.

As he reaches the bat, he notices something moving from out of the corner of his eye. Whirling to see what it is, his heart skips a beat at the sight of a small, human figure, seemingly naked, with pinkish-white skin like an albino rat scurrying down the hall toward the bathroom.

The creepiness of seeing this gives him a rush of adrenaline, and in the next instant Marsh tightens his grip on the bat and moves forward.

As he approaches the open doorway to the bathroom, he can hear a faint whispering coming from inside.

When he finally arrives at the threshold, Marsh can see a small, shadowy figure standing in the glow of the nightlight by the bathroom sink. This figure is about 2 feet tall, and as it stands with its back toward him, it continues to whisper inaudibly while appearing busy with something under the sink.

With uncharacteristic aggression, Marsh reaches out and grabs whatever it is by the shoulder and roughly turns it around.

On seeing this thing's face, Marsh recoils in horror. The figure he's holding looks just like a mini version of himself, except its skin is alabaster white and there are thin trickles of blood dripping from cracks at the corners of its mouth and eyes. The contrast of the ruby red blood against the extreme paleness of the figure's skin repulses Marsh, and in a sudden fit of rage, he drops the bat and begins strangling this creature, possessed by a murderous intent.

At that point, he suddenly wakes up and begins shouting, "NO.......NO...." into the darkness of his bedroom.

An instant later, Marsh bolts upright in bed, covered with sweat and trembling uncontrollably. Upon nervously looking around the room and seeing the furniture staring back in silence, he slowly lays down again and lets go with a deep sigh.

48

Humankind cannot bear very much reality.
~ T.S. Eliot

As he lays awake in bed, Marsh stares at the ceiling of his dark bedroom and ponders the fact that he no longer knows with any certainty what's real.

Like Brando brooding on "the horror" in Apocalypse Now, Marsh is finally coming to realize that the supposed real world he has accepted since his youth is proving to be nothing at all like he thought it was.

When his alarm finally goes off in the morning, Marsh's fear and anxiety seems to fade somewhat as the sunlight of another day offers its bright assurances through the bedroom window. By the time he's up and about, things start to seem a bit less intense, as the normal part of him once again resurfaces to take control and remind him that his dream was, after all, just a dream.

As the day progresses, this expectation of normalcy seems to gain even more traction once his mood begins to lapse into the usual *I don't like Mondays* vibe of everyone else in the streets. Upon arriving at the office, he's greeted with the usual, mindless, "Good morning, how was your weekend?" banter from Millie, making it seem as if everything is once again right with the world.

By the middle of the week though, an odd sort of grim prescience creeps into Marsh's thoughts, like a psychic in a Steven King story who starts to somehow perceive, and then directly experience, various bizarre anomalies in the world around him.

This strange new feeling that makes him start to think that he somehow knows things beyond his normal 5 senses slowly begins to expand, until Marsh actually finds himself envisioning specific events before they happen. For example, out of nowhere he has a premonition of a young man having a bike accident, and then literally witnesses the same scene a block later. Another time, he envisions a small child walking with their mother and then stumbling, falling, and crying, before seeing the exact same scene play out only seconds afterwards. The weirdest one though is when he has a vision that some unexpected money has come to him, and then arrives home later that day to find a $100 bill of monopoly money on the ground in front of his mailbox.

Rather than viewing these happenings as representing any kind of positive psychic or spiritual evolution in his life, Marsh instead feels uncomfortable about his newly emerging clairvoyance. He even goes so far as to start searching online for a psychotherapist, but eventually relinquishes the idea. Particularly after considering what a shrink's reaction might be when he tries to explain what's been occurring to him on ChatEntropy.

Refusing to let himself be seduced like an ignorant, superstitious savage by some random coincidences, Marsh instead chooses to hunker down and believe that everything he's experiencing is nothing more than simple serendipity, or even an outright fabrication of the mind.

49

As the days dissolved into weeks, and his psychic experiences continue to accelerate despite his efforts to rationalize them, Marsh is now concluding that denial is not the right way to go regarding ChatEntropy. The phenomena he's been encountering only began after he started frequenting the site, so rather than try to avoid or rebrand what is happening, perhaps he needs to embrace these experiences and see how deep the rabbit hole goes.

Even though it's been weeks since he's last logged on to the Dark Web, as Marsh heads home from work on this particular Friday, even the reticent skeptic in him is feeling a strange tingle of anticipation at the thought of returning to ChatEntropy.

After fueling himself with some dinner and a couple of beers, Marsh logs onto Tor and nervously types in ChatEntropy's address. While he waits for the browser to make the connection, he takes advantage of the time by focusing himself with a few deep, calming breaths.

Upon hitting "Start," his first chat buddy for the evening is a paunchy, middle-aged man with crazy looking eyes, medium length, tussled brown hair, and noticeably bad teeth.

"Hi," says Marsh.

"Hi," replies the man in a friendly, polite voice.

"Do you visit this site often?" asks Marsh.

"From time to time."

"Do you mind if I ask you a few questions?"

"Aren't you already?," the Man replies, as his eyes suddenly take on a playful, teasing quality.

"Yes, I am," replies Marsh with a nervous laugh. "I guess I should just continue?"

"That's up to you," replies the man.

"What's your name?" asks Marsh.

"Preston."

"I'm Seraph. What brings you to ChatEntropy?"

"Some friends have suggested that being here could help advance my work."

"Really? What kind of work do you do?"

"I experiment with sound technology."

"With music?"

"Kind of. For many years I was a recording engineer in the music business. I worked with a lot of big acts including a few Motown groups and Jimi Hendrix, but now I'm more concerned with how sound relates to time travel."

"Time travel?"

"That's right."

This certainly isn't the weirdest thing that Marsh has heard on ChatEntropy, yet it still causes him to momentarily hesitate before going on.

"Could you explain exactly what you mean?" he eventually asks.

"Sure," replies Preston, but before going on, he raises up a can of diet coke and takes a long, slow drink. Afterwards, he puts the can down, and after unleashing a loud burp, continues.

"I've just come up with an invention I call the pyramid of sound," he says. "It's designed to use the vibrations of certain kinds of music to transport whoever is listening to other dimensions in time."

"How does that work?" asks Marsh.

"The layout is simple. I've placed a comfy lounge chair in the center of 4 specially designed speakers that are positioned at the four cardinal points on the compass."

"What makes these speakers so special?"

"They've been constructed based on the specs I received from some E.T.'s who are extremely adept time travelers."

"You received this design from extraterrestrials?"

"Yup."

"How did you meet them?"

"For years I used to be the lead electrical technician on the Montauk Project.

"The Montauk Project? What's that?"

"It was a series of time travel experiments that were done by the U.S. government on an abandoned military base named Fort Hero that's located on the end of Long Island.

Marsh remains silent as Preston continues.

"In relation to my work at Camp Hero, I was taken to an underground base in Pennsylvania where the U.S. government was analyzing some remains from the Roswell crash. They wanted me to look at the control panels from the craft because they couldn't figure out how it was piloted. There was no visible power source in the thing, yet there was a wiring system. At first, I was also stumped, but then I eventually figured out that what was powering the craft was the psychic abilities of the pilots. It turns out these E.T.' s put their fingertips into some contacts on the arm rests of their seats and then their thoughts maneuvered the ship. Pretty fucking cool, huh?"

Marsh nods.

"Anyway, after I figured all this out, those E.T.' s eventually tracked me down and asked if I'd like to work with them. They knew I was an electrical engineer, and they wanted to show me how to build a speaker that could help humans time travel."

"In other words," interrupts Marsh, "you're telling me if someone sits in that chair surrounded by these E.T. designed speakers, then they'll be able to travel in time?"

"You got it," says Preston, who then takes another swig of soda and once again burps like a little kid showing off.

"Have you actually used this setup yourself to time travel?" asks Marsh.

"All the time," replies Preston.

"Where have you gone?"

"Mostly to the future."

"What's it like?" asks Marsh, feeling both curious and surprised that he's wholeheartedly buying into all of this.

"It's a lot like what you and I are doing now, but different."

"How so?"

"On other timelines you meet versions of the people you already know, but they'll be slightly different. For example, their tastes or interests may not be the same as those of the person you're familiar with, but they look just like them.

"That's weird," says Marsh.

"Quite," replies Preston.

"Just as Marsh is about to ask another question, his new chat buddy suddenly starts to act as if he can hear someone else speaking to him.

"I gotta go," he suddenly says, "They're here now and I'm being told they really need to talk to me about something."

"You mean the E.T.' s?" asks Marsh, but no sooner does he say that when he suddenly finds himself staring at a blank screen.

50

With a plump face, shaved head, and piercing eyes, Marsh's next chat buddy looks like a bigger, badder version of Uncle Fester from the Adam's Family. Clad in an English wool sport suit, a tab collar shirt, and a flower print bow tie, he nods at Marsh and in a thin, erudite British accent announces, "Do What Thou Wilt shall be the whole of the law." Afterwards, he takes a deep draw from a classic Sherlock Holmes style pipe.

Not knowing quite how to respond to such a greeting, Marsh simply watches while the man exhales a thin plume of smoke and then adds; "Love is the law, love under will."

"Nice to meet you" says Marsh, "My name is Seraph."

"Charmed to make your acquaintance," the man replies. "Even though I haven't previously had the pleasure, I have encountered a few of your brethren."

Seeing that Marsh appears confused by his comment, the man adds, "The Seraphim, of course."

Thinking that his new chat buddy is being facetious, Marsh decides to remain silent and let him continue to see where it goes.

"Let me introduce myself," says the man. "Some call me Frater Perdurabo, while others know me as the Master Therion. My surname is Crowley, as in "holy," but you may call me Aleister."

"Hello Aleister."

"You have a semitic look about you," he says. "Do you perchance speak Hebrew or know anything of the Qabalah?"

The bluntness of Aleister's remark irks him, so Marsh decides to throw caution to the wind and replies, "I haven't really pursued my semitic heritage. I had a couple of years of Hebrew school before my bar mitzvah, but it's been a while since I've even had a knish."

"Splendid," says Aleister, raising an eyebrow in amusement. "You have a modicum of wit. You also sound like an American."

"I am," replies Marsh.

"From where?"

"New York."

"I find it curious that you don't have an accent. There's a distinct absence of "dees, dems, and dose" in your pronunciations."

"Probably because I haven't used 'these', 'them', or 'those' in a sentence yet."

As Aleister takes another draw on his pipe, he continues scrutinizing Marsh as a slight twinkle in his eye reveals that he is now looking upon this young upstart much more favorably.

"How did you get here?" asks Marsh.

"By performing a magickal operation to enter a more advanced Aethyr.

"Are you aware of where we are?"

"I'm in a circle in a triangle. I notice you aren't. Are you a native of this dimension?"

"I'm not sure what you're talking about," says Marsh, adding "have you ever been on this site before?"

"No," replies Aleister, "this is my first time visiting this Aethyr."

"Does the name ChatEntropy mean anything to you?" asks Marsh.

"That is an unusual turn of phrase," says Aleister. "I would understand it as, conversing with the void. Are you a Mage?"

Ignoring the question, Marsh instead replies, "Have you ever encountered someone on this site that refers to himself as "Nameless?"

Aleister's cordial expression now changes to one of concern. "Are you familiar with the Nameless One?" he asks.

Yes, I have been trying to find him."

"You seek the Nameless One?"

"Yes, do you know where he is?"

Using his right hand, Aleister immediately begins tracing a cross in front of himself while reciting, "Atoh, Malkuth, Ve-Geburah, Ve-Gedulah, Le-Olam, Amen."

He then raises his voice and declares, "Thee I invoke, the Bornless One."

Although he's not quite sure what's happening, Marsh feels as though he is suddenly being surrounded by some type of mysterious force.

"Thou art ASAR UN-NEFER, whom no man hath seen at any time," continues Aleister.

As Marsh looks into the area of the screen beyond his new chat buddy, he suddenly notices that it is beginning to fill with a thick, white smoke. After several seconds, a form emerges out of this haze that looks like a white, life-size version of one of those faceless wooden drawing manikins that artists use for figure sketches.

"Thou art IA-BESZ. Thou art IA-APOPHRASZ," recites Aleister. As his chanting continues, the humanoid figure slowly lurches closer and closer until its midsection and shoulders fill Marsh's entire screen.

"I am ANKH-F-N-KHONSU thy Prophet, unto Whom Thou didst commit Thy Mysteries, the Ceremonies of KHEM."

As the volume of Aleister's chanting continues to rise in both volume and emotional fervor, the humanoid's hand somehow manages to pass through the computer screen and makes a forceful grab for Marsh.

Recoiling in horror, Marsh falls out of his chair and lands on the floor, after which he frantically crawls across the apartment to the opposite wall. When he finally looks back at his computer, all that's visible on the screen is the ChatEntropy home page with the word 'Next' inscribed down in the corner.

51

Sitting on the floor with his back against the wall, Marsh shouts across the room at the computer, "What the fuck was that!"

It takes a few minutes for him to regain his breath and calm down, and when he does, Marsh abruptly stands and heads to the fridge for a beer.

After drinking half of it in a single gulp, he then heads back to the computer and in one swift motion turns it off. He next crosses the room, plops down on the couch, and finishes the rest of his beer in one continuous swallow.

Afterwards, he simply stares into space, trying not to think about what just happened as he makes an effort to simply breathe and be in the moment.

It's not long before he discovers that if he only thinks about his breath moving in and out of his lungs, everything is fine. On the other hand, when his thoughts go anywhere beyond the simple act of respiration, anxiety begins to set in and there is no safe place for his mind to rest from the ghoulish onslaught he just experienced.

"It's like being caught in a creepy meme that keeps repeating itself over and over again," he thinks. "When I'm not in Chat Entropy, I'm convinced it holds some special secret that I need to know. Yet whenever I'm in it, I feel like I'm either under psychic attack or on the verge of a nervous breakdown."

"I don't know what the fuck to do anymore," he sadly whispers. A moment later he corrects himself. "Scratch that, I know exactly what to do!" With dour resolve, he proceeds to slowly get up and head back to the kitchen. "I'm going to get shit-faced," he declares, as he opens the refrigerator door and grabs another beer.

52

The harsh jangling of his phone going off suddenly introduces Marsh to the crippling tightness of a hangover, and the rudely invasive sights and sounds of the waking world.

It's Saturday morning, and with no intention of taking the call, he lets it automatically transfer to voicemail. Yet before he can turn over in bed and go back to sleep, Marsh finds himself next being harassed by an incoming text. He now looks over at the phone, thinking that perhaps it's a real emergency and he should see who it is.

Unfortunately, when he checks the text, Marsh sees that it's Sal. The message is in all caps and reads, "PIPE BURST AT 312 EAST 11thSTREET. GET HERE!!!"

"Wow," thinks Marsh, between the pulsing throbs of his headache, "that's Doug Morrison's old place." Realizing that Sal would actually come to his apartment and roust him out of bed if the situation was desperate enough, Marsh rises like a wounded soldier to face the inevitable.

It's a half-hour later when he climbs out of a cab in front of 312, followed by another frantic text from Sal. Marsh doesn't bother to read it, mainly because the one before read, "If you take any longer, I'm going to need an ark."

When Marsh exits the elevator and heads down the hall, there is a glistening puddle of water visible right in front of the door to Doug Morrison's old apartment. As he gingerly tiptoes through the open doorway, Marsh can see Sal and the Super standing next to each other inside. They are both looking up in silence as several steady streams of water come down from a collapsed portion of the ceiling.

"At long fucking last," announces Sal, as he turns and notices Marsh. "Did you stop for breakfast?"

"There was traffic. What's the situation?"

"No doubt the usual Saturday, crack-of-dawn traffic jam," replies Sal incredulously.

"We finally got the water turned off," says the Super. "Luckily, I had a big enough wrench. That main valve in the basement is a bitch to turn."

"It might have been easier if we had 3 people to do it," adds Sal, before pulling out his cell phone, tapping in a number, and walking over toward the windows in the apartment. "Is your guy on his way, yet?" he shouts into the phone, as Marsh and the Super look on like a pair of cats looking for a place to hide.

"I have major water damage on two floors and it's still coming down," yells Sal, as he squishes back and forth across the film of water that has accumulated over a sizable part of the apartment floor.

"So, when the fuck will your guy be here?!" he screams. After listening for a moment, he shouts, "Within the half-hour? Fine! I guess we'll just do a little fishing until then."

At this point, Marsh turns to the Super,"Where's it coming from?"

"Just above. Underneath us it's likely branching into other apartments because of the slant in the floor."

"What a fucking shit show," growls Sal, as he clicks off his phone. "I just had this apartment renovated and now I'm going to have to do it again."

"Where's the tenant?" asks Marsh.

"He must have slithered out just before I arrived," replies Sal.

After taking a moment to baste a little longer in his frustration and anger, Sal suddenly screams, "FUCK" at the top of his lungs. A moment later, he turns to Marsh and starts giving him instructions.

"I'm going to need you to stay here until the plumber arrives. The water for the building is turned off, so you're going to have to run interference with the other tenants in case anyone starts complaining. In the meantime, me and Aquaman here are gonna try to assess what the overall damage might be until that jerk-off plumber arrives and starts bloodletting the company's bank account."

After Sal and the Super squish out of the apartment, Marsh stands there wondering to himself how the toilet might be working after what's happened. The coffee he had on his way over in the cab is starting to make itself felt, and something is going to have to be done about it.

53

As he stands in the bathroom and listens to the music of his pee in the toilet, Marsh reaches over with one hand and angles the mirror on the door of the medicine cabinet so that he can see into the rest of the apartment.

After zipping up, he shoots another quick glance into the mirror before flushing, except this time he sees something in the main room that sends a shiver down his spine. Whirling around quickly, he thinks he catches a glimpse of the humanoid that had reached out for him when he met Aleister on ChatEntropy. Yet before he can be sure, Marsh finds that he's only looking at an empty room in a flooded apartment.

After lowering the lid on the toilet without flushing, Marsh advances cautiously back into the main room, expecting at any moment to see the humanoid again.

When he gets to the front door, he looks nervously out into the hallway before eventually re-entering the apartment and continuing to look around. His initial inclination now is to leave, but if Sal were to come back and not find him there, he'd never hear the end of it.

While Marsh waits for the plumber, he looks around the empty apartment and remembers the first time he had been there with Sal. There had been a mysterious energy in the space then that had gripped his intention, and he's sensing the same type of energy around him now. Even though there's different furniture, and a different person currently living there, Marsh can't help but feel that Doug Morrison's presence is still lingering in the space.

While Marsh is waiting, Sal calls him twice looking for the plumber, and both times his boss's disappointment is truly something to behold. After hanging up from the second call, Marsh drifts over to the windows of the apartment. and looks out at the passersby on the street. Who are these people and where are they headed, he thinks. "Where are any of us really headed," he eventually mutters aloud, hoping the plumber shows up before he has to listen to any more of Sal's bullshit.

When the plumber finally does show up, he is a diminutive and grimy looking man whose put-upon attitude gives him an ancient air, when in actuality he looks to be no more than about 40. His name is

Victor, and while Sal always complains about him, his boss continues to hire the guy. Probably because he views Sal's attitude as just more shit he has to wade through on the job. As a result, Victor isn't terribly friendly, which is evident when he ignores Marsh's greeting, and then simply grunts and heads back out the door after being told that the leak is upstairs. What a day so far, Marsh thinks to himself. "Maybe this is another level of ChatEntropy you don't have to access through the dark web.

54

It was Sal who first said out loud that the apartment was cursed, and with everything that eventually transpired regarding the flood, Marsh eventually came to agree.

For example, the day after the pipe had burst, the current tenant ended up getting seriously injured after being hit by a car right outside the building. After that, it wasn't long before they heard from his attorney that he was abandoning the apartment to move back in with his family.

In addition to the extensive plumbing work required, the flood had also affected the electrical system of the building on multiple floors, resulting in a number of serious wiring issues. When all of this was combined with the projected cleaning and renovation costs, it was apparent to everyone involved with management that the space wouldn't be rentable for a while.

During this time, there was another instance when Marsh thought he saw the humanoid in the apartment. As with the previous sighting, this one also occurred while he was zipping up after using the toilet. Similar to the first time, he had glanced over at the medicine chest and there was a reflection of the thing watching him from behind. Of course when he turned and looked into the main room, the creature was no longer there. This time however, for some reason, Marsh decided to open the medicine chest, where he was shocked to discover a huge centipede that had to be at least seven inches long on the back of the mirror. When the damn thing took a nip at his thumb as he held the inner edge of the mirror, Marsh bolted out of there.

It wasn't until weeks later, with the season's first predicted snow fall approaching, that Marsh eventually got his first full, head-on sighting of the humanoid while he was locking up after the workmen.

As with the previous sightings of the creature, Marsh was again using the toilet and looking in the mirror. This time though, rather than the damn thing running away, it instead just stood there brazenly and stared back at Marsh after he turned around.

Lasting for what seemed like an excruciatingly long time, this face-off completely terrified Marsh. His chest felt as if he had just been punched, and while his mind was racing, his body felt frozen, hollow, and immobile, like he had been out in the cold for too long.

Even though the being in front of him had no facial features, it did manage to project a sort of abstract personality as it occasionally tilted its head at odd angles, like a dog when it can't figure out what it's looking at.

After staring down each other for a bit like a couple of gunfighters in an old western, the humanoid eventually took a pair of leaden steps forward, which in turn motivated Marsh to move from the bathroom door toward the entrance of the apartment.

This inching along routine continued until Marsh was no longer blocking the humanoid's path to the bathroom, at which point the creature ran right by him like a flash. Trying to turn as quickly as he could to watch it, the thing was much too fast, and all Marsh ultimately saw was the bathroom door slamming shut behind it.

For a moment, Marsh considered going into the bathroom to confront the thing, but a sense of self-preservation prevailed, and he quickly exited the flat and locked the door behind him.

55

As Marsh exits the building and enters the nightscape of the city, he notices that the surrounding world has suddenly acquired a strange edge to it. The glow of the streetlights, the sounds of the traffic, even the faces of the people passing all seemed surreal, as if the life going on around him had suddenly changed into some kind of animated simulacrum.

These perceptions become even more severe as he descends into the subway, where the rumble of a passing train through the tunnel sounds like a crazed African drum choir. At one point, the din in the station rises to such a deafening crescendo that he can't even hear his own thoughts. When the train eventually passes, Marsh is next confronted by a homeless person on the platform who asks him for money. During this exchange, Marsh is totally convinced that this individual isn't human, particularly when they keep tilting their head in the same strange way that the humanoid had when it was facing off with him in the apartment.

By the time he arrives at his stop and is back up on the street, Marsh is moving at the accelerated pace of a man who feels like he's being followed by someone or something dangerous, but isn't quite ready yet to run for his life.

It's only after he's in his apartment with the door safely locked, that Marsh's mind stops racing. Once he has his coat off, he glances over toward Doug Morrison's computer, but then quickly looks away. Instead, he heads to the fridge and grabs a beer.

As he lays back on the couch and sips his brew, Marsh thinks he should probably order something to eat, but he really isn't hungry. Instead, he accelerates the pace of his drinking, anxiously waiting for the beer to take effect.

Even though he initially didn't want to go anywhere near the computer, after a couple of beers, Marsh suddenly finds himself on ChatEntropy again. This time, when he clicks on 'Next', he's horrified to see that the new chat buddy he's looking at is a humanoid like the one he encountered earlier. His first instinct is to shut down the computer, but when the gestures and general vibe of this faceless figure seem to be more friendly than before, Marsh finds himself starting to become curious.

At one point, when he isn't quite getting what the figure is trying to show him, the humanoid produces a hand mirror and holds it up so Marsh can see himself.

When the image looking back at him from the mirror turns out to be that of another humanoid, Marsh starts screaming and wakes up to find that he had fallen asleep on the couch.

As he looks around his apartment in confusion, first at the computer turned off on the other side of the room, and then at a slew of empty beer bottles lying on the couch next to him, Marsh groans in frustration, leans his head back, and closes his eyes again.

PART V

56

As the cleanup and renovation of the flooded apartment slogs on, Marsh's life also seems to be undergoing a transformation.

Since discovering ChatEntropy, he no longer finds himself looking at reality the same way most people would. A string of unusual encounters, both on and off the site, have managed to show him that there is a hell of a lot more weirdness out there than he ever thought possible. As a result, he now finds himself constantly on edge worrying about what the next anomaly will be to challenge his sanity.

It didn't matter that he hadn't encountered the humanoid again since his last sighting of it, the expectation that it was going to reappear at some point was taking its toll.

When he added all this to the fact that he was also being abused daily by his neurotic boss, it was no wonder why Marsh rarely felt happy anymore.

Yet in spite of the fact that there wasn't much joy or laughter in his day-to-day existence, there was absurdity, which is its own type of entertainment if you can accept the fantastically flawed logic of it all.

This type of surrealism is prominently put on display a few mornings later as Marsh walks past an art supply store on his way to work. There is an illustrator's studio depicted in the large front window, and included among the things on the artist's worktable is a small, wooden manikin that strangely enough looks exactly like the humanoid from the apartment.

The only thing that would have made this tableau seem even more bizarre given the synchronicity of the situation, would have been if the manikin had run away when Marsh looked at it.

As he continues to the office, Marsh finds himself turning repeatedly to make sure that the manikin isn't following him. Even though he feels relieved each time at not seeing it, this relief is nevertheless short-lived as a vague, abstract sense of fear continues to keep making him turn around.

When he eventually arrives at work, Marsh partakes in his usual habit of detaching himself from his surroundings as a preliminary defense against Sal's rudeness.

"Have you been to 312 yet?" yells a seated Sal from his office as soon as he sees Marsh enter.

"Good morning, Marsh," says the office receptionist, phone in hand, about to make a call.

"Good morning Millie," replies Marsh, trying not to look at Sal as his boss stares and waits for him to look over.

"HAVE YOU BEEN TO 312 YET?" yells Sal again.

As Marsh looks up to respond, Sal immediately swivels around in his chair and starts tapping out a number on his phone.

When Marsh walks into his boss's office, Sal waves him away. As he turns to leave, Sal holds the phone against his chest and yells after Marsh, "Close the door behind you."

After halting his forward progress to turn and pull the door closed, Marsh next heads toward the main door of the office while saying over his shoulder to Millie, "If he asks, tell him I'm on my way to 312."

When he turns to make sure she heard him, Millie waves in acknowledgement without looking up from her call.

Luckily, 312 is within walking distance, yet before he even makes it to the corner Marsh's phone goes off with a text. It's Sal asking if he is on his way to 312.

While Marsh waits for the traffic light on the corner, he starts to text Sal back, but before he can begin typing, another text from his boss comes in with a list of instructions on what to do when he arrives at the apartment.

There is a good coffee place on the corner just before 312, so on his way, Marsh makes a quick pit stop. While the guy is preparing his order, Marsh receives another text from Sal. "Are you at 312 yet?" Since there is no right answer to that question before he actually steps into the apartment, Marsh simply ignores the message, gets his coffee, and leaves.

312 is literally 2 doors away from the coffee place, and as Marsh waits for the elevator in the lobby, his phone chimes with another text from Sal, "Where r u?"

An additional text comes in as he's letting himself into the apartment, but Marsh doesn't bother to check it.

"I can tell already this is going to be a memorable day," he remarks to himself, as he looks for a place to put down his coffee so he can finally text Sal back.

57

Surprised to see a folding chair, card table, and laptop in the otherwise empty apartment, Marsh makes his way over to them and puts down his coffee.

After he texts Sal, his mind flashes back to the first time he had entered this space and spotted Doug Morrison's laptop in the very same place. As he cautiously looks at the computer on the table, the door of the apartment suddenly opens, causing him to whirl around.

It's the electrician, and he seems as surprised as Marsh to see anyone else in the space. On recognizing Marsh, he simply says, "Hey," and continues past him to the computer.

"I thought you were done in here," says Marsh.

"Yeah...." says the electrician, leaving the rest of his sentence to dangle in mid-air as he sits down and starts doing something on the computer. His name is Mose and he's been working with Sal's management company since long before Marsh's time.

"Is everything okay?" asks Marsh.

When Mose doesn't respond, Marsh continues. "Does Sal know you're here?"

The mention of Sal's name usually gets an immediate response from anyone who's ever dealt with him before, and this time is no different as Mose looks up from what he's doing and responds, "Not yet."

Before Marsh can say anything else, Mose adds, "He will though, as soon as I know what's going on."

"Is there a problem?" asks Marsh.

"I'm not sure, give me a minute," says Mose, continuing to focus intently on his computer.

As Marsh plays out in his head the likely conversation between himself and Sal when Mose is ready to tell him what's going on, he drifts to the window and stands there sipping coffee while watching the passersby down on the street.

He's absently staring at someone picking up after their dog when Mose finally announces from the other side of the room, "I got it."

"What?" asks Marsh, as he turns and walks over toward Mose.

As Mose explains in layman's terms what's happening with the wiring in the apartment, Marsh watches him closely. "He's probably not that much older than me," Marsh thinks, "yet there's something about him that makes him seem like he's ancient."

Mose had taken over his father's electrical contracting business, and from everything Marsh had heard about the old man, he and his son were exactly alike. From the tufts of black hair on the back of their respective necks, to the perpetual five o'clock shadows they each spoke through like they were laconic hit men for the mob.

Marsh also admired that Mose was one of the only people he knew that didn't give a shit about what kind of mood Sal was in. That more than anything impressed Marsh about the guy.

"I can't say that I fully understand what you just said," remarks Marsh when Mose is done, "so let me get Sal on the phone and you can explain it to him yourself."

"Sure, says Mose. "I'm not going to do anything before I get an okay from management. Technically, Marsh was management, but they both knew that the money flowed from Sal and no other.

"Hey Sal," says Marsh, turning his back on Mose as soon as his boss is on the line. "Mose is here now at 312 and I think you should hear from him about what he wants to do."

"What the fuck? Why didn't you tell me that gorilla was there?" shouts Sal.

Without a word, Marsh hands his phone to Mose.

"Hey Sal."

As Mose sits there and delivers his explanation to Sal, Marsh marvels at the electrician's imperviousness to Sal's rudeness, like a bear that isn't hungry as it watches nearby campers.

When Mose hands the phone back to Marsh, Sal is already talking. "He's gonna replace a junction box."

"I know," said Marsh. "Do you need me to stay here?"

"Would you have any idea what the fuck he's doing?" comments Sal sarcastically.

"Not really."

"So then why would you need to be there? Just tell him to call you when he's done and then you'll go over and see if the lights work when you turn them on."

"Should I come back to the office," asks Marsh, like the straight man in a comedy routine feeding lines to the star."

"Sure," answers Sal. "I always like to see what you're doing to earn the money you're getting paid. You can help Millie with some paperwork."

After hanging up, Marsh looks at Mose and wonders if the electrician might have seen anything weird since he's been there.

As he turns to exit the apartment, Marsh chuckles quietly to himself as he imagines the humanoid being too intimidated to approach Mose.

"Let me know when you're done," announces Marsh over his shoulder on the way out. "You have my number, right?"

"Yup," replies Mose, without looking up from what he's doing.

58

When Marsh arrives at the office to find Sal unexpectedly gone and Millie out to lunch, an idea occurs to him as he sits down at the spare computer station.

What if the humanoid I saw wasn't only connected to that strange character named Aleister on ChatEntropy? What if Doug Morrison also encountered it? We both used the same computer, and the second time I saw that creature was in Morrison's old apartment.

Marsh didn't think that Mose, or any of the other workmen had likely seen anything, but what about the tenant that had succeeded Morrison? The flood happened while that dude was living there, plus his supposed accident and subsequent breaking of the lease seemed a little too coincidental. It was also weird that Sal didn't try to get anything out of the guy for moving out early.

After a quick consult of the company database, Marsh is easily able to find the information he's looking for. The tenant who succeeded Doug Morrison in the apartment is named Victor Neuberg.

Single and 40 years of age, Mr. Neuberg, was gainfully employed as a digital illustrator for an international design company with an office in New York City. Aside from his own cell number, the emergency contacts listed are a Mr. and Mrs. Carl Neuberg of Islington, England. "Well, well he's a Brit," thinks Marsh.

For a second, he considers the possible blow-back if Neuberg should be annoyed at receiving a call from him, after all, it could mean his job if Sal got wind of it. As he reviews the relative pros and cons of doing this deed, Marsh finally convinces himself that locating a missing person is more important in the grand scheme of things than losing a job he hates.

Marsh tries the cell number first and after several rings, a soft-spoken British voice answers.

"Hello," replies Marsh. "Is this Mr. Victor Neuberg?"

"May I ask what this call is in reference to?"

"Are you Mr. Neuberg?"

"Once again, who's calling?"

"My name is Marsh Simon and I'm phoning from Copperfield Properties in New York City. I'm the assistant managing agent of the building you used to live in located at 312 East 11th street."

"Why are you calling?"

"Is this Mr. Neuberg?'

"First tell me what this is about.

"Fair enough," says Marsh. "If you are Mr. Neuberg, this call is not regarding anything legal and you're in no trouble whatsoever. I'm just calling to ask a few questions about your experience living at 312 East 11th street."

"My experience? Could you be more specific?"

"It's documented in our records that there was extensive damage to your apartment due to a flood that occurred as the result of a plumbing problem in the building. At first, you moved into a hotel room at my company's expense, but then you broke your lease after experiencing an accident shortly thereafter. Specifically, it says you were struck by a car. Is all this correct so far?"

“If you’re calling to try and exact some sort of penalty for breaking the lease, my attorney has already dealt with the matter.

“You’re absolutely right, I’m aware that everything has been taken care of and you have no legal or financial liability whatsoever. All I want is to ask a few questions about your experience of living in the building, both before and after the flood.”

“Why?”

“I don’t know if you’re aware of this, but the tenant who lived in the space prior to you disappeared during the pandemic under circumstances that appear suspicious.”

“No, I wasn’t aware of that.”

Well, since you had a pair of unusual incidents occur to you while living in 312 that we already know of, the flood and your accident, I was wondering if you had experienced anything else out of the ordinary that was disturbing to you in any way?”

After a short silence, Neuberg replies, “What the hell are you asking me?”

"I realize that this may sound weird, but did anything of a metaphysical nature ever happen while you were living in the apartment?"

Without responding, Neuberg immediately hangs up.

"So much for that," says Marsh to the empty room.

Just as he begins thinking about a few places he might send his resume to, the office phone suddenly rings.

With no one else there, Marsh answers the call. "Copperfield Properties. How can I help you?"

"Can I speak to Marsh Simon please?"

"Mr. Neuberg?"

"I wanted to make sure that you're who you said you were."

"Not a problem. I understand. I did ask you quite an unusual question and you had every right to be suspicious."

"I'm still suspicious, so why don't you just ask me exactly what you want to know, and I'll see if I can answer."

Sensing he might be hung up on again, Marsh nevertheless figures, "The hell with it," and proceeds to ask, "Did you ever encounter a being in your apartment that looks like a life-size version of one of those wooden dolls that artists use for figure drawing?"

When an answer isn't immediately forthcoming, Marsh braces himself to be disconnected again, yet a moment later he's shocked to hear a soft, clear "Yes," on the other end of the line.

Another moment passes before Marsh continues, "Okay. Can you tell me anything else?"

"What would you like to know?"

"Exactly what you experienced, whatever it was."

"Well, it was a day or so after the flood, and I was staying in the hotel. I had only gone back to the apartment to see if I could get some more of my things. You know, clean clothes, some other stuff. I was packing up what I could find that wasn't wet when I suddenly felt something behind me and turned."

As Neuberg pauses, Marsh can feel him struggling with what to say next.

"There was this thing standing there," he says. "It was what you described, like one of those drawing dummies that artist's use. It just stood there looking at me. Its head was moving around a bit, like it was taking me in, but it had no face or expression."

Neuberg stops again, but this time Marsh immediately asks, "What happened next?"

"It moved like nothing I've ever seen. It was so fast. Before I knew what happened it was in the bathroom and the door shut behind it."

"What did you do after that?" asks Marsh.

"I don't know. I guess I was in shock. I don't believe I'm telling you all this. I also can't believe I'm actually admitting it to myself out loud. I feel crazy. How could anything like that possibly happen?"

"That's okay," replies Marsh. "I felt the same way when I first saw it. If it helps, I can't believe I had the stones to even ask you about this. I mean it sounds like we're both looney tunes. Yet if it happened to both of us separately, maybe it's real?"

Before Neuberg can reply, Marsh adds, "If you don't mind my asking, how did your accident happen?"

"As you might imagine, I ran like hell out of that place and the next thing I knew something really hit me. After that, I woke up in the hospital. At that point, there was no way I was going back to that apartment ever again and I didn't care how much legal hell I had to go through."

"Since you brought it up, do you mind if I ask you a few things about the legal aspects of you leaving the apartment?"

"That depends."

"Can you explain to me why my company didn't hold you liable for the remainder of the lease?"

"I didn't speak for several days after what I just described," says Neuberg. "My parents got me an attorney, as well as a doctor and a psychiatrist to confirm that I was in no shape to be on my own for the foreseeable future. I guess your company just figured suing me wouldn't be all that productive for them."

"Thank you for telling me all this," says Marsh. "It explains a lot. "I also saw in your records that your parent's contact address is listed as Islington, England. Did they come all the way over here when your accident happened?

After a short pause, Neuberg replies, "I think I've shared enough for the time being."

"Are you in England now?" asks Marsh.

Without answering, Neuberg quickly changes the subject. "So, you saw that thing too?" he asks.

"Yeah, I did."

"What did you do?"

"Pretty much the same as you, except I managed not to get hit by a car on my way out. Which is a miracle if you ask me, because I was in a daze much like you were."

"Why did you look me up?" says Neuberg.

"Well, it turns out I've been trying to figure out why the tenant before you disappeared. What I've found so far has opened a whole can of worms that eventually led to everything we've just been talking about."

"Interesting," replies Neuberg mysteriously.

Neither man says anything else for a few moments, which makes Marsh figure that it would probably be a good time to make an exit, so he politely ends the call.

After hanging up with Neuberg, Marsh leans back in his chair and exhales a weary, "Cheers mate," before slipping into a deep daydream that's only interrupted when Millie returns from her lunch hour.

59

When the work week is finally over, Marsh is relieved to be back in his apartment with some sushi and a six pack of craft beer.

After finishing a brew, he starts on the sushi, and by the time the second beer is finished, he eventually has ChatEntropy up and running on the laptop.

When he cracks open a third beer, Marsh is staring blankly at the ChatEntropy home screen while reviewing where he is in his search for the elusive Doug Morrison.

“If truth be told,” he thinks to himself, "I'm no closer to finding my person of interest than when I first started. On the other hand, I have managed to see more than a couple of things I’ll never be able to unsee. Oh yeah, and there’s some interdimensional creature from inside Doug Morrisson’s computer that seems to be following me.

It strikes Marsh that maybe doing a flow-chart of where this journey has led him so far might be helpful, but the beer has him feeling nice and he resigns himself to just sitting there and thinking.

Easily the weirdest thing about the whole adventure up until now has been the humanoid. As his third beer dwindles, Marsh thinks back to the first time he encountered it. That guy named Aleister seemed to conjure it out of thin air.

A quick Google search on his phone for the name Aleister yields a top result of Aleister Crowley. "Crowley as in Holy," Marsh remembers him saying. I guess this must be the guy.

"Another dead one," Marsh thinks, as he recognizes the profile photo of Aleister on Wikipedia and then sees that Edward Alexander "Aleister" Crowley (1875-1947) was an English occultist, philosopher, ceremonial magician, poet, painter, novelist, and mountaineer. He also founded a religion called Thelema, was a spy for MI6, and consorted with E.T.'s.

"He sounds like fucking James Bond," thinks Marsh. "I guess it makes sense that he was a ceremonial magician. After all, it did seem like he conjured that humanoid from out of the smoke. What was it he said that seemed to make that damn thing appear?"

It takes a moment, but the expression "Bornless one" eventually pops into Marsh's head. " That's right," he thinks. "I mentioned the handle 'Nameless', and then Aleister started in with that incantation about the 'Bornless one'. Who the hell is the Bornless one?"

As he goes to get his fourth brew, Marsh tries to work out a theory for the data he's accumulated so far.

"If Aleister conjured up that humanoid thing to specifically come after me, then how did Neuberg see it in his apartment unless he also encountered Aleister and just didn't tell me? But how? For Neuberg to have met Aleister he would also have to know about ChatEntropy. Maybe Neuberg is also a ChatEntropy ghoul that can cross into the real world like a humanoid?

He continues thinking.

So, what's the thread connecting Aleister, the humanoid, Morrison's old apartment, Nameless, and Neuberg? I don't know how they all fit together, but the loose end seems to be Neuberg. None of it seems to work if there isn't some kind of connection between him and the rest of it.

"There has to be something connecting all this shit," Marsh thinks to himself, but with the weight of the work week still heavy on his shoulders, as well as the tipsiness he's feeling from the beer, he's unable to formulate any type of theory before lazily drifting off to sleep.

60

Having decided to sleep in, Marsh is lying in bed and staring at the ceiling when the thought suddenly crosses his mind to do a Google search for the name Victor Neuberg.

"Of course," he says, and then quickly jumps out of bed and goes across the room to his laptop.

"How crazy is all this shit going to get?" he thinks, as a dark sense of foreboding seems to be watching over his shoulder while he enters Victor Neuberg's name into the search bar.

A moment later, Marsh is confronted with an antique looking photo and the following description.

"Victor Benjamin Neuberg "6 May 1883 – 31 May 1940 was an English poet and writer. Neuberg was born into an upper middle-class Jewish family and raised in Islington, a suburb of London, England.

"Since I've never met him, I don't know if the guy I talked to looks like this photo," thinks Marsh.

"Maybe he's not another dead one, although coming from Islington is an ominous coincidence."

After quickly finishing with Neuberg's early life, Marsh reads something next that startles him. It turns out that in 1906, when Victor Neuberg was 25, he came in contact with one Aleister Crowley, who had read some of his poems in a literary magazine known as the "Agnostic Journal."

"He's a Chatentropy ghoul too," whispers Marsh to himself. "That motherfucker lied to me."

The article then goes on with a full description of the deep relationship that developed between the two men. Running the gamut from the literary to the mystical, and even the sexual, their association culminated in a fantastic magical ritual they performed together in the North African desert while attempting to invoke the demon of the abyss known as Choronzon.

According to the article, the ritual Crowley had used to lure the demon into the sacred triangle was known as "The Invocation of the Bornless One."

At this point, Marsh stops reading.

“Neuberg wasn’t surprised by the humanoid in his apartment,” he says aloud. “He invoked the damn thing. He was able to because he knew the Bornless ritual. The real question though is how is Victor Neuberg still alive in the real world?” With no answer to that question, Marsh resumes reading.

Following their ritual, the two men then immediately split company, with Neuberg needing several months to recover from the emotional and psychological ordeal of the experience.

“I guess he didn’t learn his lesson the first time,” thinks Marsh, “so the stupid shit goes out and makes the same dumb ass mistakes all over again; first trusting Aleister, and then invoking demons.

At this point, Marsh sits back, shakes his head, and wonders if it would be a good idea to start drinking before breakfast. “The Bornless One indeed,” he whispers, suddenly realizing that there’s currently nothing for him to drink in the apartment.

61

Half-way through both the afternoon and a six-pack, it dawns on Marsh to try and call Neuberg again. He picks up his cell, but then immediately puts it down and instead begins rehearsing what he might say to the empty apartment.

"Neuberg, my good man," he announces in a mock British accent, "did you ever know a bloke by the name of Crowley, as in Holy? I just read that you and he had a little sojourn down in North Africa together back in the early 1900s. You supposedly invoked a demon by the name of Choronzon. Does that ring a bell? By the way, I also have this theory that the humanoid didn't surprise you in your apartment after the flood. I think you invoked the damn thing. After all, you and old Aleister called on nasty little things like that all the time, didn't you?"

As the empty beer cans on his desk stare back in silence, Marsh gets up to go to the bathroom.

While standing over the bowl, he tries to imagine how Neuberg would react to the accusation of being an invoker of demons and almost 150 years old.

Plopping down again in front of the computer with another designer brew, Marsh prepares for his next foray into the twilight zone, a.k.a ChatEntropy. Yet instead of firing up the machine, for the moment he simply stares at his dim reflection on the sleeping screen.

After drinking and daydreaming for a few minutes, Marsh eventually gets things going while thinking to himself, "I wonder what'll be waiting on there this time?"

Once he's on the site, Marsh hits "Next," and then waits for the screen to come on like a bored kid stuck inside on a rainy day to watch T.V.

For some reason, the connection is slow, and when the new screen finally arrives, rather than finding himself confronted with some ChatEntropy character to challenge his sense of reality, Marsh is instead presented with the view of an empty apartment.

Perhaps it's because he'd been day drinking, but it takes Marsh a few seconds before he realizes that what he's looking at on the screen is the interior of his own apartment.

"Motherfucker," he declares in amazement.

Even though he doesn't see himself on the screen, Marsh nevertheless waives at the view of his empty room.

"This is fucking cray-cray," he says, with a half-snort of nervous laughter. "The only thing missing is me."

Unable to move forward with any coherent line of thinking about what he's now looking at, Marsh's awareness turns within, and he suddenly realizes that he needs to pee again.

On his way across the apartment to the toilet, Marsh looks up, and what he sees through the open bathroom door stops him in his tracks. Staring back at him from the mirror covering the medicine chest is the face of the humanoid he had previously encountered at 312.

Seeing this thing in the mirror scares the living shit out of him, and for several moments Marsh stands there frozen with his heart racing wildly. It is only when one of the thing's arms starts to reach out beyond the surface of the mirror and materialize in real time, like it is grabbing for him, that Marsh's instinctive fight or flight mechanism kicks in and he rushes over to slam the bathroom door shut.

"This is way too fucking much," he shouts at the closed door, while at the same time knowing deep down inside that the craziness is just beginning.

Still needing to pee, Marsh begins pacing around the room like a caged animal. At one point, he glances over at his computer, but the view of his empty apartment on the screen has now been replaced by the ChatEntropy homepage. Looking back at the closed bathroom door, he can't help wondering if he'll ever be able to use the facilities in his apartment again.

Feeling like there's no safe space anywhere for either his thoughts or person, Marsh grabs a coat and quickly exits the apartment.

62

Arriving out on the street, Marsh sees that the night has surreptitiously arrived, bringing with it a sunset sky and the glow of the streetlights.

Like a spooked cat, he makes his way down the sidewalk, hoping to lose his fear and anxiety among the throngs of people and traffic along the avenue.

As he moves back and forth through the passing pedestrians like a skier doing a slalom, Marsh is driven by a deep panic that eventually pushes him down into the subway.

Without consciously intending to, he eventually ends up coming out of the train to find himself only a couple of blocks away from 312 East 11th street. A few minutes later, as he stands and looks up at the façade of 312, Marsh imagines the humanoid locked in the bathroom of Doug Morrison's old apartment as it tries to get back to wherever it needs to go through the mirror. Maybe Neuberg is also there. Good old 150-year-old Neuberg, consort of Aleister Crowley, invoker of demons.

It crosses Marsh's mind to go to the office, but what would he do there? Maybe he could research the various tenants that lived in Morrison's apartment before he moved in? After nervously grasping in his pocket for his key ring, Marsh turns and starts walking quickly toward the Copperfield office.

63

After using the bathroom, Marsh is now seated at the spare desk in the office as he searches through the tenant history of Morrison's apartment. Under the cold glow of the overhead fluorescents, he can feel himself teetering on the boundary between the reality he's always known, and the insanity of a dimension that contains things like ChatEntropy and humanoids in mirrors.

It feels like a lifetime has passed since he first went to Morrison's apartment with Sal, but in actuality it has only been a little less than a year. In fact, as he goes through the records of the preceding tenants, he realizes that he had started his job only about a year after Morrison had moved into the place. Before that, there had been a steady stream of one and two-year leases for the space that were started and terminated without much fuss or anything unusual.

After searching for a while, Marsh eventually arrives at the conclusion that there isn't anything particularly exciting or weird to be found regarding the history of the apartment before Morrison. As he leans back in his chair, he starts to review the events that have brought him to where he is now. All this weirdness and tumult was happening because he wanted to find someone who had disappeared. Yet the way things were going, it probably wouldn't be too much of a stretch to think that all this strangeness might ultimately end up with his own disappearance. After all, those humanoids had to be after something, otherwise, why would they be following him?

As these thoughts continue to swirl in his head, they are soon accompanied by the beginnings of a headache and thirst that makes Marsh realize that if he doesn't have another beer soon, the hangover process is going to start to take over the situation.

64

Back on the street, Marsh heads to the train while trying to think of a place to go and grab a beer.

Ordinarily, he'd just pick up a 6-pack at a supermarket somewhere and simply head home, but the thought of the humanoid in the mirror has him feeling that perhaps a bar with other actual humans in it would be better right now.

Within a couple of blocks of his apartment, Marsh comes upon a little French bistro that he'd been in before for happy hour. A quick peek inside reveals that it's not too crowded, so without any further ado, he sidles in.

On surveying the scene, he takes a seat at the bar between some people clustered together in a small gathering, and a single woman drinking alone.

After ordering a beer, he then lets himself settle into the atmosphere of the place as he focuses his attention on his drink. There's a mirror behind the bar, though he initially avoids looking at it for fear of what he might see. When he's finally calmed down enough to scan his surroundings, Marsh is surprised to find that the woman at the end of the bar is checking him out. Wearing a sleeveless down vest and turtleneck sweater, she appears to be your typical out of town transplant with long, straight brown hair and a thin, pretty face.

Instinctively Marsh nods at her, which elicits a smile in return. Suddenly, before he realizes it, he's on his feet and standing next to the young woman's barstool

"Hi, I'm Marsh," he says, glad to finally have something pleasant to focus on. "Would you like some company?"

After a shy smile, she says, "Sure," and then looks straight ahead as he climbs onto the stool next to her.

"By the way, I'm Persephone," she says, now looking at him.

"Persephone, huh? "I've always wondered about giving children mythological names, but in your case, I can see the resemblance."

After hearing something that she didn't quite expect, Persephone smiles. "Really? That's funny because the goddess Persephone is from Ancient Greece and I'm from Kansas City. "

"Kansas or Missouri?"

"I'm a Chiefs fan, so figure it out."

"A Missouri girl." He nods. "Well, I guess you "showed me."

She smiles at his pun. "Why do you think I look like Persephone?"

"You have that plutonian glow."

"Plutonian glow? Oh my god, now you're trying way too hard."

"Yeah, I guess so," he says, smiling sheepishly. As he finishes his drink, Marsh checks to see where Persephone is with hers. "What are you having?" he asks.

"Chardonnay."

After calling over the bartender and placing their orders, Marsh and Persephone continue talking amidst the noise of voices and house music filling up the bar.

“So, are you from around here?” she asks.

“Yeah, a couple of blocks over, just off York.”

“Then we’re neighbors. I’m over on Second Avenue. What do you do?”

“I’m a managing agent for a residential apartment building.

“Oooh, when I’m ready to get out of my roommate situation, maybe you can help me find an apartment.”

“That can be arranged,” replies Marsh.

Before he can continue, the bartender arrives with their drinks.

Once the bartender is gone, Marsh asks, “So, what do you do?”

“I’m a nurse.”

“Nice. Where?”

“NYU Langone.”

"Then why a roommate? Nurses do alright."

"It's all about work now for me. I decided on a share so I could set myself up with some savings for the future."

"To a lady with a dream," he says, raising his beer.

"Praise the goddess," she replies, as she touches her wine glass to his bottle of beer.

After some more small talk, Marsh again notices that they're both running low. "Are you ready for another?" he asks.

"This one's on me," she says, and looks over to the bartender.

"I can sense the healing energy around you already," quips Marsh, as the bartender acknowledges Persephone's signal and gets to work on their next round.

65

With the moon now high in the sky over the buildings, Marsh and Persephone slowly stroll along 1st Avenue as the traffic rolls uptown like a river of red lights under the streetlamps.

"So, where are we headed?" asks Marsh.

"In case you forgot, I have a roommate," she says.

"And which roommate will the lady choose for this evening?" says Marsh, with an insinuating grin.

"Since I live in the other direction, which one do you think?" she asks.

"I would be honored," he says with great sincerity.

"Such a gentleman," she remarks with a smile, after taking his arm and leaning into him as they walk.

"This street is me," he says, when they reach the next corner.

As Marsh unlocks their passage through the double entry doors of his building, Persephone asks, "do you have any pets?"

"Nope, just me."

"Excellent" she says. "I'm allergic to animal hair. I mean I love kitties and little dogs, but they will literally kill me if there isn't any Benadryl available."

Once they enter the apartment, Marsh's eyes are immediately drawn to the closed bathroom door, which instantly induces panic as he remembers the humanoid and worries about Persephone eventually asking where the john is.

As if she were telepathic, Persephone drunkenly announces how badly she has to pee. This forces Marsh into being chivalrous, as he quickly heads to check out the bathroom before allowing his date to use it.

Whispering to himself, "fuck it," he nervously pushes open the bathroom door and flips on the light. To his relief, all he finds is an empty room and his own reflection in the mirror.

"Are you using the bathroom?" asks Persephone, now right behind him.

“Uh, no. I was just showing you where it is,” he replies.

“Thank god,” she says, and pushes by him before abruptly shutting the door.

Relieved at the bathroom being empty of humanoids, and inspired by Persephone’s presence, Marsh is glad to have someone there with him, especially a total hottie like her. Suddenly the bathroom door flies open, and Persephone enters the main room announcing, “I feel sooooo much better!”

There’s nothing that will clear your mind of worry like something to keep you busy, so as Marsh and Persephone get started expressing their affections for one another, the idea of the humanoid still being there never once occurs to Marsh for the remainder of the evening.

66

As Marsh turns over in bed, the first thing he sees upon waking is Persephone getting dressed in the morning light coming through the window.

"You're leaving," he groans, rubbing his eyes and yawning.

"I have a shift in a little while. I didn't plan on not going home last night and I need to get my stuff before I go to work."

"You mean like your stethoscope?"

"Funny," she says, "you better hope you don't get sick at NYU.

"Okay, well, would you like some coffee or something before you go?"

"No, that's okay. I'm good. I have some coupons for Dunkin Donuts."

Now fully dressed, Persephone turns and heads to where she threw her coat when they first arrived. In response, Marsh gets up, pulls on some shorts, and stumbles over to show her out.

"You don't have to get up, I can let myself out."

"So, what is this," asks Marsh, stopping short and rubbing his sleepy eyes, "a hit and run?"

"No, it's just that I have the kind of job one can't be late for," she says, putting on her coat.

"I get it," replies Marsh tiredly, "saving lives and all."

"Hey, I loved last night, and it sounded like you did too, but I work crazy hours, and I just don't have space in my life for ……"

"Meeting my family, getting married, and having kids?" quips Marsh.

As Persephone's eyes widen in surprise, Marsh calmly adds, "Just kidding! Got you though, didn't I?"

"That's what I get for offering my body in exchange for the possibility of getting a cheap apartment," she says, while turning and heading for the door.

"Can we at least be friends on Facebook," he calls after her, "so I can stalk you in a socially appropriate way?"

"I have to go save lives now," she says over her shoulder, undoing the deadbolt and opening the door to the apartment. Before leaving, she turns and blows him a kiss.

After the door closes quietly behind her, Marsh refastens the deadbolt and then shuffles off to the bathroom to pee.

As he opens the door, the thought of the humanoid suddenly comes to mind, causing him to hesitate for an instant. Doing a quick scan of the bathroom, Marsh is surprised to see a phone number emblazoned in red lipstick across the mirror.

917- 547- 167♥

"One digit short of true love," he mutters, while positioning himself in front of the toilet. "I guess Persephone has gone back to the Kingdom of the Dead after all".

67

After a shower and some breakfast, Marsh eventually looks out the window and notices that the morning light, which had so beautifully enveloped Persephone while she dressed, has since turned into a gray and overcast day.

Turning from the window, he then looks across the apartment toward the bathroom, where the partial phone number Persephone had left is visible on the mirror.

At the time, he thought he was lucky that the humanoid didn't interrupt his liaison with her, yet now he realizes that feeling safe in his own apartment shouldn't be a matter of luck.

"I can't always be looking over my shoulder and repeatedly worrying that some fucking creature may invade my space," he thinks.

Energized from the previous night, Marsh now once again finds the fortitude to fire up his computer for another round on ChatEntropy.

While he waits for the machine to go through its appointed tasks, the relaxation from his recent liaison starts to fade as Marsh frustratingly ponders the fact that his search for Doug Morrison has pretty much led to nothing more than an entry into another dimension that he wished never existed.

Nonetheless, once the familiar screen appears, Marsh is stubbornly ready to dive back into his search.

"It ain't over till it's over," he whispers to himself defiantly, then clicks "Next."

Marsh's newest encounter on ChatEntropy turns out to be an ancient looking Asian man with long white hair, white eyebrows, and a white goatee. He's wrapped in some type of ornate robe, and on his head is a small, black pillbox hat. The energy this old dude projects is so thoroughly saturated in peace and quiet that when Marsh eventually speaks, he finds himself whispering.

"Hello, my name is Marsh. I'm wondering if you can help me."

After the old man nods silently, Marsh continues.

"I have been looking all over the internet for a lost friend. He goes by the handle of "Nameless." Have you ever encountered someone like that?"

As the old man stares deeply into Marsh's eyes, the younger man eventually perceives a soft voice inside his head saying, "Why do you seek this Nameless one?"

Not seeing the old man's mouth move and not actually hearing his voice initially confuses Marsh, yet before he can question what's happening, the soft voice in his head continues.

"A way can be a guide, but it is not a fixed path."

"I don't understand," replies Marsh, referring to how the old man is somehow projecting his voice telepathically into Marsh's consciousness.

"When you seek to understand, you are merely searching for the divinity within you do not recognize," whispers the voice in Marsh's head.

Besides the anxiousness he's feeling at having this old man somehow enter into his thoughts, Marsh is even further confused by the nature of his statements.

“Relax,” he now hears the old man telling him. “Just listen to your awareness and then think about what you’d like to reply.”

After taking a deep breath, Marsh thinks to himself, “I’m looking for a man named Douglas Morrison who refers to himself as Nameless. Can you help me?”

The old man smiles. “Now we are both of one mind,” hears Marsh inside his head, after which the old man lifts a small cup of tea to his lips.

When he is done drinking, the old man puts down the tea, followed by Marsh hearing a noise in the apartment that causes him to nervously turn around.

When there’s nothing there, he looks again at the old man. “What is the faceless thing that’s appearing in my apartment?” he thinks, surprised at his newfound ability to converse telepathically.

“Hell is a hall of mirrors in which we do not recognize ourselves,” echoes the soft voice of the old man inside Marsh’s head.

“Are you suggesting that humanoid thing is a part of me?” says Marsh.

There is another noise in Marsh's apartment, except this time when he turns, he sees an apparition of the old man standing in front of the bathroom door. Once again, he hears the old man's voice inside his head, "It is all in your mind, you just don't know how large your mind is."

When the apparition suddenly fades away, Marsh turns back to his computer, where once again the old man is on the screen. "Be careful of what you are looking for," he announces inside Marsh's head, "It can only be just what it is.

68

Before Marsh can respond to the old man, he suddenly finds himself looking at the 'Next' button at the corner of the screen.

"How inscrutable," he thinks, disappointed at the old man's summary dismissal of him. After a resigned sigh, Marsh slowly moves the cursor and clicks "Next."

When the new screen appears, Marsh is stunned by what he sees.

For the second time, he finds himself looking at a view of his own apartment, yet once again, he's not in it.

Just as he had done when this occurred previously, Marsh looks back and forth between what's on the screen and what is visible behind him in the apartment to confirm that they are one and the same.

"This just keeps getting curiouser and curiouser," he says aloud to himself.

It's then that he remembers the last time this happened he had also seen the image of the humanoid in the bathroom mirror.

Getting a strange inkling that he should go to the bathroom and check if the humanoid is there, Marsh rises and heads to the john. On the way toward the closed bathroom door, mixed feelings of both anticipation and dread swirl around in his head.

After he opens the bathroom door and discovers there's no humanoid in the mirror, Marsh turns and heads back to the computer, where he eventually sits and resumes looking at the view of his apartment on the screen.

As he stares into the live picture of his empty room, the image in front of him suddenly begins to flicker, followed by everything going black. A moment later the image returns to the screen, but then it quickly goes black again and stays that way for a bit.

Assuming that the network connection has been lost, Marsh works to try and get it back, when suddenly the screen returns all by itself. This time though, besides just showing the interior of his apartment, there is also a humanoid sitting there and looking at him.

Even though a shock of fear shoots through him at seeing this thing again, Marsh doesn't try to shut off the computer. Instead, he sits there in silence and looks back at the blank, yet strangely evocative face that's taking him in.

After a brief staring contest, Marsh begins to realize that the longer he looks at it, the less this humanoid seems like something alien or threatening. In fact, he even starts to think he can see something accessible in the blank, yet surprisingly attentive face.

At that point, the computer screen begins to flicker again, subsequently causing the image of the humanoid to disappear and reappear several times. When the connection to ChatEntropy finally stabilizes, Marsh eventually finds himself confronted with a new image that literally makes his heart stop. No longer is he looking at the face of a humanoid staring back at him from the screen. Instead, Marsh finds himself now looking directly into the face of his exact double.

PART VI

69

Even though he's totally freaked out at seeing another version of himself, Marsh can't help but stare at the computer in amazement. As he does, a sense of indecision takes root within him that alternates between succumbing to this onscreen doppelganger's weird seduction, and listening to an inner voice that's telling him to avert his eyes and focus on something real before it's too late.

Just as it starts to feel like he's about to blend into the image he's looking at, Marsh notices the appearance of his double begins to change. Its eyes appear to be growing larger by the second, except the bigger they become, the less they resemble eyes. Instead, the gaze of his double has now transformed into a pair of immense, mirror-like portals, which Marsh can feel himself beginning to get sucked into.

As he falls further into this space, Marsh suddenly senses that he's becoming engulfed in a denser and more threatening situation, like he's been dunked into a jacuzzi and is getting sucked down into the warm, churning water.

The next thing he knows, Marsh wakes up from what seems like a deep sleep to hear a doorbell ringing. As he turns over in bed and looks around in the dark, his attention is drawn to a crack of yellow light coming from under what looks like a closed door on the other side of the room.

Once his eyes are used to the darkness, Marsh is surprised to see that he is in his boyhood bedroom. As he looks around, he recognizes the pictures of his favorite baseball players on the wall and the small desk in the corner by the window where he did his homework. The next thing he becomes aware of are a pair of voices speaking on the other side of the closed door. One voice sounds like his mother, but the other is a man's voice he doesn't recognize. He can't quite make out what they're saying, so after throwing back the covers, Marsh tiptoes to the door of his room and opens it. As he squints into the brightly lit, short hallway that leads to the kitchen, he can hear the TV playing in the living room to the left, along with the voices of his mother and the man coming from the front door.

It's at this point Marsh notices for the first time that his body and clothing don't match his adult self. To his amazement, he realizes that he is a boy dressed in pajamas. After puzzling over this incongruity for a moment, his attention is suddenly drawn back to the sound of the man and his mother talking.

He still can't fully hear what they're saying, yet from his current vantage point he can now see the open front door of the apartment. Beyond its edge, the back of his mother's figure is visible as she talks to the man's voice in the hallway. As Marsh creeps closer to the door, he can clearly feel from the sound of his mother's voice that she's upset.

As the man she is talking to responds, whatever he is saying is suddenly interrupted by the static from some kind of radio or walkie-talkie.

"IS HE DEAD?" his mother suddenly shrieks over the static, sounding more like an animal than a human.

"I'm afraid so, Ma'am," says the Man. Marsh can then hear his mother start to wail uncontrollably as his awareness is mysteriously transported to another location. In this new place he is still a young boy, except now he's wearing winter boots and a heavy coat over his pajamas. He is standing next to his mother and there are two policemen with them. They are all together in front of a closed door marked 'Morgue'. To the left and right of the door, a dingy looking, institutional green hallway extends in both directions under the harsh glow and loud buzzing of fluorescent lights. The four of them remain there in silence until the closed door unexpectedly opens and a doctor in a white coat emerges.

"Are you here to identify the body?" he says to the group.

"Yes, this is the wife," replies one of the cops.

Marsh's mother now starts to cry again while shaking her head back and forth. "I can't, I can't," she keeps mumbling.

As the two policemen awkwardly look at each other, Marsh's mother suddenly collapses to the floor, after which one of the cops helps her up and guides her over to a nearby waiting area.

"Someone has to identify the body," says the doctor to the other cop.

As Marsh looks at the doctor, he can't seem to make out his face, only a mop of hair, glasses, and his white coat.

"I can't, I can't," Marsh's mother keeps saying from down the hall.

"We'll go in with you, Ma'am," says the cop that's with her, but she only shrieks back, "I SAID I CAN'T! LEAVE ME ALONE!" She then puts her face in her hands and starts to cry uncontrollably.

The doctor now looks to the other cop standing alongside Marsh and repeats, "The body has to be identified."

"What about the kid?" suggests the cop, nodding toward Marsh.

After taking a moment to assess Marsh, the faceless doctor eventually looks at the cop and says, "Why not? It looks like that's all we got."

A moment later, Marsh finds himself being led by the doctor through the door marked 'Morgue'. Once inside, he sees a flat, silver metal table with something on top of it covered by a white sheet. At the far end of this table, Marsh can see a pair of bare feet sticking out from under the sheet, as he suddenly starts to notice how cold it is in the room.

"Just say 'yes' if you recognize who it is," says the doctor, as he pulls back the sheet to reveal Marsh as a grown man lying there dead.

70

Seeing himself dead in the morgue jolts Marsh awake, where he now finds himself once again sitting in front of his computer. Except now, rather than looking at his doppelganger staring back at him from the screen, he's instead confronted by the smiling face of a silver-haired, middle-aged man.

"Wow, you look like you've had a rough trip," says the man.

It takes Marsh a few moments to get his bearings, but eventually he realizes he's back on ChatEntropy after spying the 'Next' button down in the corner of his computer screen. It's then that he remembers he had been looking at his doppelganger.

As Marsh sits there trying to sort all this out in his head, the middle-aged man merely sits back and watches. When Marsh finally comes out of his fog and looks directly at his new chat buddy, he can't help but notice how this dude appears to project a much nicer vibe than what he's used to on this site.

After sitting there for several more moments in silence, Marsh eventually asks the man, "Who are you?"

"Ah, I thought you'd never ask. My name is Timothy, Timothy Leary."

The name sounds vaguely familiar to Marsh, but in his present state of mind he just can't seem to place it. "Have you ever come across anyone in this place calling himself "Nameless?" Marsh asks.

"Nameless? That sounds a little ominous. Let's start instead with who you are."

"I'm Seraph," replies Marsh hesitantly, remembering that he doesn't want to give his real name to anyone on ChatEntropy.

"Seraph? That's quite a trippy name. I'm sure you're aware it describes a form of angelic being in Christian mythology. In fact, the Seraphim symbolize light, ardor, and purity. Does that describe you?" he adds with a sly grin.

Encountering someone on ChatEntropy that doesn't exude an obvious level of decay or malevolence intrigues Marsh. As a result, he's not quite sure how to deal with Timothy's friendliness.

For another few seconds the two men simply stare at one another, until Marsh breaks the silence by asking, "How did I get here, with you?"

"All I know is that I was meditating and suddenly you were sitting there in front of me."

"What was I doing?" asks Marsh.

"Nothing much," Timothy replies. "You seemed a little disoriented and I just wanted to get a feel for where you were coming from. I figured that you'd likely been through some strange shit and were naturally strung out about it. After all, reality isn't necessarily the neat little setup we're socialized and educated to believe it is."

"Have you ever been here before?" he asks Timothy.

A corner of the older man's mouth turns up into a half-smile as he replies, "It feels like I've always been here. I've been wandering the Bardo now for a while trying to see what my next birth will be."

"The Bardo? What's that?"

"In Tibetan, the name Bardo Thödol literally means, 'Liberation by Hearing on the After-Death

Plane'. It's all laid out clearly in a work called, *The Tibetan Book of the Dead.*"

"I think I've heard of that," replies Marsh, adding, "Are you saying we're in a book?"

"No of course not," answers Timothy with a giggle. "That would be a little bit too freaky, you know, like *Mist* by Unamuno. Anyway, the *Book of the Dead* is more than just a book. It's a road map of the metaphysical planes that exist between human incarnations."

After a momentary pause, during which Marsh's face reveals his obvious confusion, he eventually musters up a response, "How do you know so much about this bardo stuff?"

"*The Tibetan Book of the Dead* opened the door to my true life's work," says Timothy.

"What do you do?"

"I'm a philosopher, psychologist, writer, and explorer of universal truth."

"That sounds kind of new-agey."

"For some people it can be that kind of trip, but my work is actually based on ancient wisdom that's designed to help us find our way back to the core of all being."

At one point in his life, Marsh might have rolled his eyes at this sort of metaphysical claptrap, yet coming out of this man's mouth it instead had a ring of validity to it.

"I can tell you one thing for sure," says Timothy, "This level of the Bardo doesn't have the usual darkness or despair of the lower planes. Been there, done that, and I can tell you it's no fun. I guess we're meeting here now because both of us must have evolved to the point that we're ready to deal with the next step in our evolution.

When Timothy finishes, Marsh finds himself surprised to hear anyone on ChatEntropy say something affirmative, even if he doesn't quite understand what Timothy is talking about.

"If you don't mind my asking, what brought you here?" says Timothy.

"I'm looking for someone who disappeared," replies Marsh.

"You mean the Nameless guy you asked about before?"

"Yeah."

"It sounds like *The Long Goodbye* by Raymond Chandler. How did he disappear?"

"I don't know, but I think it had something to do with this website we're on now."

"A website?" says Timothy, sounding confused for the first time in their conversation. "That's a different way of looking at it, though I guess it's not such a stretch from the ancient Tibetan belief of layered realities that merge together into a formless void."

"You mean to tell me we're not having this conversation in cyberspace?" says Marsh.

"Ultimately, who knows?" replies Timothy. "After all, our brains are essentially soft computers, and consciousness is a universal neural system just like the internet. Either way, we're always in some sort of consciousness paradigm, right?"

"Wait," says Marsh, "Aren't you looking at me right now through your computer on a website called Chat Entropy."

"ChatEntropy? Wow, that's a groovy name. It sounds like some kind of alternate reality."

"It is. It's a chat site on the Dark web."

"The dark web? Whoa! That's totally radical. I've been out of the computer tech scene for a while, but back in the day the cyber gurus in California were always theorizing about the possibility of a distributed, decentralized, information storage and retrieval system that could anonymously share files online. Do you know who it was that actually managed to do it?

"Offhand, no, but I'm sure you could look it up online. But wait a minute. You haven't answered my question. I'm seeing you on my computer right now, aren't you seeing me on a computer too?"

After averting his eyes for a moment, Timothy looks back at Marsh and hesitantly answers, "No, I'm not seeing you on a computer."

"Then how are you seeing me?"

He shrugs, "Sort of like a holograph floating in front of me."

"What?"

"That's the way I see everything now," says Timothy. "It seems like everyone becomes naturally clairvoyant after they……" He stops.

"After they, what?" asks Marsh.

"After they've evolved in their spiritual comprehension of things," replies Timothy, and then quickly changes the subject. "You know it didn't click before when you first mentioned it, but now that I think about it, this Nameless dude you're talking about makes me think of the Bornless One from Western Magick."

"What?! Where did you get that?" asks Marsh, with an edge to his voice.

"Get what?"

"That expression, the Bornless One, where did you get it?"

"Well, I first heard of it after reading Aleister Crowley, but I subsequently found out that he got it from the rituals of the Golden Dawn."

"Aleister who?"

"Aleister Crowley. He was a metaphysical philosopher, writer, and ceremonial magician who lived in the early 20th century."

"I know. I've met him here on ChatEntropy. He set some kind of humanoid looking creatures on me after shouting some ritual mumbo jumbo about the Bornless One."

"Are you telling me you met Aleister Crowley on this site that you think we're both on now?"

"Yeah."

"And he set *what* on you?"

"These humanoid creatures. They look like the flexible wooden dummies that artists use for figure drawing. Aleister was reciting some ritualistic mambo jumbo and one of those dummies materialized and reached right through the computer screen for me. Since then, these things have continued appearing not only on my computer, but from time to time in my daily life as well."

Timothy chuckles, "That sounds like something Crowley would do, but I don't think his actions had the dark intent you're assuming."

"Are you trying to say he was doing me a favor?"

"He may have been sending you a guide."

"A guide? To where?"

"Maybe it was supposed to be your guide through the bardo. Many get lost on this journey and there's no guarantee of making it through."

Suddenly, something seems to dawn on Marsh. "Wait," he says, "Haven't you been saying the Bardo has to do with the dead?"

As Marsh nervously continues, Timothy's smile now disappears for the first time since they've met. "If we're not on ChatEntropy, but in this Bardo you keep talking about, how did I end up here? I mean, if that's where we are."

Timothy now looks at Marsh compassionately, as the younger man stares into his eyes looking for an answer.

“How could we both be in the Bardo if I’m on a computer and you’re not,” asks Marsh, trying to sound confident.

Timothy remains silent as Marsh once again searches in the older man’s eyes for an explanation.

“If it’s true we’re both in the Bardo,” concedes Marsh nervously, “then that would mean I couldn’t be online. If that’s the case,” he hesitates and looks off in the distance. “Does that mean I’m...”

“More than you think you are?” says Timothy, managing another smile. “Don’t be so bummed out. The journey through the Bardo is essentially a metaphor. It’s symbolic of the psychological and spiritual pilgrimage we each must make through our inner darkness so that the soul can find its highest evolution.”

Instead of feeling encouraged by what Timothy just said, Marsh instead remains silent as he tries to come to grips with what it seems to mean to be in the Bardo.

71

"So, what made you want to search for this guy Nameless?" asks Timothy, hoping to lift Marsh's spirits. "Was he a friend or a relative?"

"No, it was all pretty anonymous," says Marsh listlessly." I just happened to work for the landlord that took possession of his old apartment after the police declared him missing."

"Do you have any idea how he disappeared?"

"It looked like he might have died of COVID. It was an easy assumption to make at the time since the news was reporting there were a lot of anonymous corpses that weren't being identified."

"COVID?" repeats Timothy.

Marsh looks at him with disbelief. "Yeah, the worldwide pandemic that recently killed millions of people."

"Wow. One of those finally came back again to get humanity."

Not wanting to ponder why Timothy would make such a strange remark, Marsh drifts back into a depressed silence as the older man tries again to keep the conversation going. "So, what was it that motivated you to actually start searching for this Nameless cat? Whatever you found out must have been interesting or you wouldn't have continued looking."

Hesitantly, Marsh replies, "I thought it was weird that his computer was still on when we took possession of the apartment. After all, the place was vacant for almost a year.

"That's definitely unusual," says Timothy.

"After doing a little investigating into his computer with a friend," continues Marsh, "we eventually discovered the last place he visited online was called 'ChatEntropy'; the site I've been telling you about."

"I must admit, this all sounds extremely trippy," says Timothy.

Suddenly, Marsh nervously asks, "Tell me the truth, are we really in this Bardo thing now?"

"The subtle realms are hard to put a definitive label on," replies Timothy hesitantly. "This location could be anywhere, or nowhere. For now, I'm sensing that we're together at this point in time to help each other get to wherever we need to migrate."

"What do you mean, wherever we need to migrate?" asks Marsh. "What the fuck has happened to me?!"

Timothy's expression now turns serious again, as he looks deeply into Marsh's eyes.

"I think it's time to turn off your mind, relax, and float downstream," he says softly.

"What?" demands Marsh, as a wave of deep emotion starts to well up within him. "What the fuck are you telling me? WHAT ARE YOU SAYING?!"

While Timothy gazes at him, Marsh watches the old man's face start to fade and shift on the computer screen as his image begins rolling and twisting like a ribbon of smoke coming from an incense stick.

Feeling a sudden shock of fright move through him like a flash of lightning in a storm, Marsh's body initially tenses up, but then he slowly slumps forward and covers his face with his hands. A moment later, a trickle of quiet tears starts to fall between his fingers like the first drops of a coming rain.

"How can we become still?" asks Timothy rhetorically. "By moving with the stream," he adds, trying to sound as cheerful as possible as his face on Marsh's screen once again pulls together into the image of a recognizable person. "You've merely reached a transition, my dear Seraph. Try and look at it this way, whatever follows is what's going to set you free."

Without picking up his head, Marsh mumbles into his hands, "But I'm still young. I'm not ready to let go of everything."

"You're only as young as the last time you changed your mind," repliesTimothy.

72

When Marsh eventually stops crying, he slowly picks up his head and emits a long sigh. Embarrassed at his outburst of emotion, he refrains from looking at the computer screen and sheepishly excuses himself, saying to Timothy, “I need to use the bathroom. I’ll be right back.”

As he walks across the apartment, Marsh can hear Timothy’s voice echoing softly inside his head just like the Old Asian man’s had. “If you don’t like what you’re doing, you can always pick up your needle and move to another groove.”

In the bathroom, Marsh leans over the sink and splashes cool water onto his face, after which he turns, takes a towel, and dries himself. It is only as he’s about to leave the bathroom that Marsh dares to stare into the mirror to check if there is a humanoid looking back at him.

When there isn’t, he takes a deep breath and heads back out to the computer. As he sits down, Marsh is surprised to see that Timothy’s smiling face is no longer there. Instead, he finds himself confronted by a totally white screen.

"Have I imagined everything that's just happened," mutters Marsh, feeling almost relieved at the possibility he might have been dreaming again.

A quick look at the router on the other side of the room near the TV shows that everything is still connected to the internet, yet when he looks back at the screen there are no identifying marks or prompts to indicate he's still online.

After sitting in front of this white screen for a while, Marsh finally decides to get up and fix himself something to eat. Yet on arriving in the kitchen, he's suddenly surprised to find he has no appetite. What he has mistaken for hunger instead seems to be the gnawing emptiness of some deep, abstract space within him.

He eventually drifts over to the window, where he absently-mindedly pauses to look outside. It surprises him to see that it's pitch black out there. "Damn," Marsh mumbles to himself, "I must have been online a lot longer than I realized. I forgot I started doing this shit early this morning."

Since there is nothing to see beyond the window except complete darkness, Marsh figures that maybe a streetlight on the block has gone out, so he turns and makes his way back to the computer to check if anything has come up on the screen.

As he sits down, the face of an adult male somewhere around his own age unexpectedly appears on the computer screen in front of him. The surprise of seeing this stranger makes his heart skip a beat, as Marsh suddenly gets the feeling that his long search over the last several months is about to come to an end.

"Hi," he says nervously to the person in front of him, "My name is Seraph."

"I'm Nameless."

73

Some journeys, like a train, plane, or taxi ride, simply lead you to a new destination and something else to do. Others, like Marsh's search for Doug Morrison, lead you into much deeper places, perhaps even the unexplored parts of yourself.

As they sit and face each other, Marsh expects to hear the person he is looking at tell him the solution to a great mystery. After all, his search for Nameless has led him to places he never even knew existed, both in cyberspace and beyond. Yet despite all that has happened to him on his journey, Marsh is nevertheless surprised to find himself tongue-tied by all the questions he feels a need to ask. On the other hand, Nameless simply sits there like a serene Buddha, comfortably enfolded within the calm of silence.

"What happened to you," Marsh finally blurts out, instantly regretting the impatience and frustration he feels in his voice, like an exasperated parent needing a definitive answer as to why their child has just done something stupid or dangerous.

"I could ask you the same thing," replies Nameless.

After thinking about it for a second, Marsh flatly replies, "I guess so, but I was the one looking for you."

"Do you know what you've found?"

For an instant Marsh seems puzzled, but then responds, "I found you. I found this place we're in now, and I expect I'll eventually find out what all this means. But at the moment, I could use some help from you."

Nameless nods in acknowledgement, and then replies, "To be honest, the simple fact is that I was only looking for a distraction from my life when I accidently discovered a crack in the universe and fell in. Ever since then, I've learned that reality is more than any of us ever imagined. I've also realized how we all have our own hells to pass through and our own truths to discover."

"Did you die of COVID?" asks Marsh, unable to think of anything else.

"I can't say for sure what happened to me. I never felt sick. I simply saw another version of myself, and reality changed."

For an instant, Marsh remembers seeing another version of himself as well, but before he can dwell on it, he compulsively says to the man in front of him, "Do you miss being Doug Morrison and the world he existed in?"

"Do you miss being whoever you were before you became Seraph?"

"I still am that person. Seraph is just a handle for the places I needed to go looking for you."

"Are you sure you're still that person? In fact, did you ever really know who that person was?"

The gravity of exactly where he is suddenly places its bony hand on Marsh's shoulder and the chill of it reverberates through his whole being. "Is it really a matter anymore of just shutting down ChatEntropy and then being back in my apartment?" he thinks.

Marsh begins to wonder if things have finally gotten to the point where he will never be able to leave this unexplainable void that he now finds himself in. As the bleakness of this thought sits in his gut like a case of indigestion, Marsh also wonders, "What has the purpose of all this been?"

As if Nameless was psychically attuned to Marsh's thoughts, he suddenly declares, "It's no longer a matter anymore of just shutting down a program and going back to what you know. By the time you arrive in this place, you're not looking at a program on your computer anymore. In fact, it's no longer even about you, at least not what you thought you were."

"What is ChatEntropy?" mutters Marsh involuntarily, suddenly surprised at the strangeness of his own voice, as if he were hearing it for the first time.

Nameless smiles. "ChatEntropy is the reality of consciousness. When most people think of their awareness, they're only considering what their five senses are revealing to them. That, and what they've been taught. Your search for me woke you up from the somnambulism that your socialization and education had induced in you. It's that limiting mindset that makes you believe only a small sliver of this infinite universe is real. Now you've seen otherwise, and you can't ever go back to not knowing."

"So exactly where are we now?" asks Marsh.

"Eternity."

"What does that even mean?"

"You're at the entrance to the endlessness beyond what we experience as ourselves. It's the infinity of possibilities that exist beyond material reality. From here, all consciousness keeps evolving toward a higher vibration that eventually dissolves into a single pure awareness of everything.

"Then what would happen if I shut off this computer where I'm seeing you?" asks Marsh, surprised at how frightened he is at hearing his own question.

"I'm not seeing you through a computer," answers Nameless.

"I've heard that one before," says Marsh nervously, "What does it mean?"

"It means it's your turn to find out for yourself."

As Marsh sits back to ponder everything they've been discussing, he suddenly hears the sound of a rising wind coming up all around him. At first, the incongruity of hearing such a sound startles him, yet as the noise of the wind gains in volume, Marsh can't help but notice how the air surrounding him is starting to feel lighter, fresher, and suddenly very intoxicating.

When he focuses again on the computer, Marsh now notices that the image of Nameless has disappeared from the screen. In its place, he now finds himself gazing into the face of a very formidable looking, and very beautiful black woman. She is wearing a maroon-colored bandana wrapped around her head, and from underneath it a long mane of thick, black hair cascades over her bare, muscular shoulders. Almost instantly, Marsh finds himself totally mesmerized by this woman's gleaming eyes. As he becomes lost in them, she begins speaking in a strong, sultry voice that seems to originate from inside his head, just like those of the old Asian man and Timothy had earlier.

"Do you know where you ah?" she asks in a lilting, African patois.

As Marsh tries to think of how to answer, the Woman continues.

"You have reached Iku," she says, "and I am here to welcome you."

"What is Iku?" asks Marsh.

"You may think of it as a gate," she replies. "It is where you will leave behind one way of being and encounter another."

"But I'm still in my apartment."

"Your mind has brought all that with you for now, but soon you will no longer need such illusions."

ChatEntropy had been weird before, but something about the countenance of this stunning looking woman is making Marsh feel like he's entered entirely new territory. As he thinks about simply turning off the computer and leaving the apartment, the woman resumes speaking.

"You cannot turn away from what is happening," she says. "Your Ifá quest has brought you to this place between worlds, and you must continue."

"Who are you?" asks Marsh, a part of him wanting to know, but another part of him wanting to stall until he is sure of where all of this is going.

The woman's stern face unexpectedly breaks into a smile, yet despite the sparkle of her sensuous white teeth, her grin exhibits an edge that does not suggest mirth.

"My name is Oya and I am the wind. I am also the keeper of this gate you must now pass through."

"I would prefer to remain where I am," replies Marsh.

"You ah already the consequence of a choice, and you must continue. Do not worry. I am adept at this. Many pass this way."

"Where am I going?"

"For now, you will wait in a place we call Amalla. I think you would call it death, but that is a term you don't really understand. Once you pass through the gate, what happens next will be up to your Emi, or what many think of as the "soul."

At this point, a fearful panic begins to stir in the pit of Marsh's stomach."

"You have walked your path to this point, and you must continue," says Oya. "Your Kadara, or destiny, is waiting.

When he looks away like a child trying to resist their bath time, Oya's tone turns to one of a mother's guidance.

“Call upon God, and the Lord shall save thee,” she whispers to him. “Evening, morning, and at noon, pray, and cry aloud; and he shall hear your voice. He will deliver your soul in peace from the battle that was against you, for there were many with you.”

Suddenly, the image of Oya disappears from the computer, leaving Marsh once again with a blank, white screen to look at. The crisp, cool quality of the air around him also starts to fade, as the voice of Oya suddenly announces itself again from inside his own thoughts. “Go ahead child, shut down your instrument.”

Following this command like a subject listening to their hypnotist, Marsh slowly reaches over and turns off the computer. A moment later, the machine instantly evaporates into the space around him, like the wind returning to the nothingness from whence it came.

As he continues to stare at where the computer had been, Marsh now suddenly finds himself face-to-face with the images of his departed father and mother. A wave of emotion engulfs him as they float there in front of him, a pair of full body holographs wearing outfits Marsh had remembered from an old picture. While he tries to process what he is seeing, Marsh instinctively glances down at his hands, which he now sees have become transparent, making him realize that he too has become a holograph.

While the trio float there and stare at one another, his parents smiling at him like Marsh remembered from his boyhood, he notices that he can no longer feel his body. It is as if he is now nothing more than an awareness or an essence drifting in space.

It's hard to say exactly when the moment arrives that Marsh ceases to be his respective point of view, yet once it happens, every coordinate of reference he has been aware of instantaneously disappears into an infinite and endless light.

PART VII

74

The garbled voice and crackling static from a police radio fills the hallway, as Tank and a pair of uniformed cops stand there watching the building superintendent try to open the door of Marsh's apartment.

Tank hadn't spoken to his friend for a couple of weeks before finally calling Marsh at work to see if he might be interested in meeting up for a drink. At first, the earful of angry complaints that he received from Sal made Tank want to hang up, but once the conversation eventually toned down, everyone involved agreed that something bad had likely happened and the police should be notified.

They had been friends since childhood, and as Tank leaned against the wall watching the Super try one key after another, he silently chastised himself for not trying to contact Marsh sooner.

"I should have *known* something was up with that dark web shit when I didn't hear from him for a while," thinks Tank.

When they eventually gain access to the flat, the cops commence to huddle up, while the Super takes a call on his cell and Tank drifts over to a desk where he sees the computer he had wiped clean for Marsh a few months earlier.

The machine is still open and covered with dust. When Tank leans over to touch the keys, the jarring voice of one of the cops warns him off, "Don't touch anything in here until we take a look around first."

Tank nods in acknowledgement to the officer and then drifts toward the windows against the far wall while the cops start nosing around the apartment.

As he stares down at the street below, Tank is already planning what he will do when he gets his hands on that computer and can check out what his friend was up to on the dark web. He doesn't want to jump to any conclusions just yet, but Tank has some strong suspicions that his friend had somehow gotten in way over his head with the stuff he was doing on ChatEntropy.

The possibility that Marsh might have ended up the same way as the dude he was looking for made Tank feel more than a little uneasy, especially as he thinks about what might lay in store for him if he picks up where his friend had left off.

75

"Are you the one that filed the missing person report," says one of the cops, interrupting Tank's thoughts.

"Yeah," replies Tank, turning from the window and looking at the officer.

"What is your relation to the person missing?"

"We've been friends since childhood."

"When did you last see or speak to your friend?"

"I last spoke to him a few weeks ago. It's been a bit longer than that since I last saw him."

"Why do you think he's missing? Maybe he just went away for a while."

"I called his job, and they haven't heard from him either."

At this point, the other cop comes over and whispers something in the ear of the officer Tank is talking to.

When the cop looks back at Tank, he asks him, "Can you give us the name of his employer?"

"Sure, Copperfield Properties."

"Is it here in Manhattan?"

"Yeah."

"Do you know the name of somebody I can talk to?"

"Sal. He's the owner."

"Got it. Does this Sal have a last name?"

"Sorry, but I don't know it."

"Have you ever talked to this guy Sal?"

"Yes. We both agreed that I should call the police."

As the cop continues jotting down information, Tank says, "Is it okay if I ask you something?"

Once he's done writing, the cop looks up. "Sure, go ahead."

"Would it be okay if I took my friend's computer with me when I go?"

The two cops exchange glances, and then the other one asks, "What do you need it for?"

"I thought I'd look over his internet searches to see if there's anything that might show what he'd been up to."

"Maybe it would be better if our tech guys did that."

"I'm a professional computer tech," answers Tank, as he hands his business card to the officer. "I've consulted with the N.Y.P.D. on a few occasions. I have a contact at the 17th precinct over on 51st street; Detective Lieutenant Rowe. You can call him if you like. He'll vouch for me. Of course, if I find out anything, I'll share it with you guys asap."

The two cops look at one another. "Sure, give me a minute," the one cop says, as he looks at Tank's card. "I'll give him a ring."

As the cop with Tank's card steps away to make his call, the other one resumes looking around the apartment.

In the meantime, Tank returns to the window and becomes lost in his thoughts as he looks down at the street.

"You're good," says the cop, as he comes up behind Tank a few minutes later. "The Lieutenant told me you're the man when it comes to this kind of stuff. He said you should take the computer and let us know what you find."

He gives Tank a card. "When you're ready, call this number and ask for Sargent Sanders, he'll be coordinating things"

"Thank you," replies Tank, "I'll be in touch."

76

By the time Tank gets back to his office it's well into the evening and everyone is gone for the day. After checking to see if he has any messages, he then goes and sets up in the same workroom he had brought Marsh to all those months ago.

Everything goes smoothly, and within a short time Tank acquires the link that Marsh had used for the dark web version of ChatEntropy.

As he sits there and hovers the cursor over the link, a flurry of thoughts fill his head.

His friend is the second person to have disappeared in relation to this site. Even though Tank didn't share Marsh's attraction to mysteries, when a pair of real people disappear after having been on a notorious chat site, it does manage to give one serious pause. What exactly had his friend gotten himself into?

The pragmatic part of Tank was telling him to steer clear of the whole business, yet his love for his friend was arguing back that you don't just let a buddy disappear without doing something about it.

If he needed them, the N.Y.P.D would be there to back him up. After all, Tank had helped Lieutenant Rowe on several occasions and they had developed a pretty good professional friendship.

Besides, what did he have to worry about? Computers had always been a safe place for him. Whether he was a kid playing video games, a college punk hacking into different sites as a practical joke on the establishment, or a professional working for commercial clients, cyberspace was somewhere he had managed to find his place in the world.

“This is just another hack,” he tells himself, yet he also remembers thinking the same thing when he had first helped Marsh, and now his friend is gone.

It hadn’t occurred to him before, but as Tank clicks on the link to ChatEntropy, he suddenly realizes that the alternate reality he had always thought was so cool in the Matrix was now perhaps something real that he could actually get lost in if he wasn’t careful.

As he sits there gazing at the ChatEntropy home page and its ominous-looking ‘Start’ button down in the corner of the screen, Tank begins to feel a creeping anxiety. “What if I’m entering into a completely new reality with nothing but yesterday's tools and yesterday's concepts at my disposal," he thinks to himself.

After sitting with that thought for a moment, Tank takes a deep breath, exhales "Fuck it" in a soft voice, and clicks 'Start', completely unaware of the humanoid figure that's watching him closely from an oblique angle just outside the door to the work room.

ABOUT THE AUTHOR

T.C. Eisele is a Professional Astrologer, Author, Poet, and practicing oenophile based in New York City.

His books include *Psychic Reading* (A Play) 2017, *Liber Tao* (A New Tao Te-Ching) 2015, *The Exalted Man* (Haiku) 2014, and *Liber Quantum* (Non-fiction) 2011, all from Rebel Satori Press, plus *Modern Magickal Keys* (Non-fiction) from Abramelin Press in 2004. A book of poetry, *Graphic Reflections,* will be forthcoming from 9VT/5 Press in 2026.

He has also been a frequent contributor to numerous periodicals and online magazines including, *The Astrology Quarterly, Cosmopolitan Online*, *Poetry East*, and *The New York Quarterly*.

www.ingramcontent.com/pod-product-compliance
Lightning Source LLC
La Vergne TN
LVHW012041160826
845678LV00014B/2666

* 9 7 9 8 9 9 1 3 9 4 2 9 1 *